Slaves
for the
Isabella

Julia Edwards was born in 1977. She lives in Salisbury with her husband and three sons, and sometimes feels outnumbered.

Slaves for the Isabella is the fifth book in *The Scar Gatherer* series, seven adventure novels about time-travel. To find out more, please visit: *www.scargatherer.co.uk.*

Slaves
for the
Isabella

For Sam,

Best wishes,

Julia Edwards

Julia Edwards

Published in the United Kingdom by:

Laverstock Publishing
129 Church Road, Laverstock, Salisbury,
Wiltshire, SP1 1RB, UK

First printed November 2017

Cover design by Peter O'Connor
www.bespokebookcovers.com

ISBN: 978-0-9928443-7-0

For more information about the series, please visit
www.scargatherer.co.uk

For Benjamin,
the peaceful

ACKNOWLEDGEMENTS

As ever, I am indebted to my husband and my parents for their support. My particular thanks this time go to Mike Rendell, writer of the Georgian Gentleman blog – which features, among many other entertaining pieces, an excellent post on toilets! – and to Christine Huard, a former Ofsted Inspector with an interest in Georgian history. Their knowledge of this period helped me to make this book much more accurate than I could have achieved alone. I would also like to thank my friend, Judy Edwards, whose first-hand knowledge of tall ships helped me to bring the *Isabella* to life. Thanks also go to the staff at the Georgian House Museum in Bristol, who answered umpteen questions about domestic life in the 1790s, and to the children and staff of Wilton and Barford Primary School, who watched over the writing of this book and gave me their feedback on the draft version. Any errors that remain are my own.

1

"I'm starving!" Joe said. "Can we get something to eat?"

His dad looked round. They were standing in a deserted street with a church at one end. Dad was pointing at the spire, half hidden in fog. "I thought you liked history!" He sounded slightly hurt.

"I do," Joe said. "But not churches and not before breakfast! Sorry," he added.

"You're right," Dad said, letting his arm fall. "What twelve year old is interested in churches? I was getting carried away. It's being back in Bristol that does it. Your brother wouldn't have let me go on like that!"

As though in answer, the church clock struck: half past eight.

"If Sam was here," Joe said, "he'd be in bed for another hour at least!"

Dad grinned.

Joe gazed down the street. It was flanked by

gracious stone buildings, ghostly in the February mist. The one right next to them was a café. "How about there?" he suggested.

"It looks a bit coffee-and-sandwiches, don't you think? I fancy a proper fry up! There used to be a good greasy spoon down this way."

Joe groaned inwardly. 'Down this way' was going to mean hustling Dad past a lot of old buildings. It was like being in a toyshop with a small child. And the annoying thing was that usually, it would be fine. In fact, if they'd only had breakfast before they came out, this might have been the perfect place.

He dug his hands into his coat pockets. In one was the scrunched up chain of the St. Christopher Dad had given him when he and Mum split up. The circular pendant had got buried in fluff in the corner of the pocket. Joe ran his thumb over the picture on it. Nobody else would be able to tell by the feel of it what it looked like. But he'd held it so often that he knew which bit was St. Christopher's head, and which was his feet, tramping through the river carrying the baby Jesus.

Tradition said a St. Christopher should protect the traveller who wore it. Joe smiled to himself. This one hadn't protected him at all! In fact, it had put his life in danger several times during the last year and a half!

He thought back to the first time he'd ever dropped it, on the mosaic at Fishbourne Roman

10

Palace. He'd had no idea what was about to happen. It had taken him ages to realise it was the St. Christopher that had spun him back into the past. Even now, he hadn't managed to pin down when it would weave its magic.

Sadly, it seemed to have stopped working altogether. He'd tried it in the Peak District in October, and in Oxford in December. But nothing had happened. Getting it to touch an old bit of ground or stone without anyone noticing, and without losing it, was so difficult, he was nearly ready to give up.

Just one more time, he decided. If it didn't work in Bristol, he wouldn't try again, even though that meant he wouldn't see his friend from the past again. Something fluttered inside him. He'd really missed Lucy after the Great Fire of London, more than he was willing to admit to anyone including himself. But then he'd started secondary school, and what with all the homework and the clubs, he'd stopped thinking about her quite so much. Maybe it was time to forget her. The fluttering continued. He ignored it.

"This is St. Nicks Market here," Dad said, as they walked down the street. "You know, the market building was once the Exchange."

Joe rolled his eyes. Dad just couldn't resist! "This is where the merchants did their trading in the eighteenth century," Dad went on. "These bronze posts are called the Bristol Nails." He pointed at the nearest one. There were four in total, spaced out along the front of the market. They were about as tall as Joe's chest, with flat, round tops.

"They're not very nail-like, are they?" Joe objected. "Nails don't have bulges in the stems."

"I suppose not," Dad agreed. "But that's what they've always been called. The person selling would spread his wares on top of the nail for the buyer to inspect, and if the buyer was happy with them, he would put his money down to seal the deal. They say that's where the phrase 'paying on the nail' comes from."

Joe nodded. He thought about the height of the nails. This would be a brilliant place to try his St. Christopher. He was sure he could press it against one of the bronze heads without Dad noticing. Even better, if he held on with his other hand, he might be able to stop himself from collapsing as he came back into the present afterwards, if by any chance the St. Christopher worked.

"It's a shame the market's not open yet," Dad was saying. "It would have been nice to wander through it. Perhaps we should come back after breakfast."

Joe glanced around. Right now, there was nobody nearby. Later, there were bound to be more people around. It might be a lot more difficult. Perhaps his stomach could wait.

He held his St. Christopher tightly in his right hand. Dad looked upwards.

"You see the clock up there –"

But Joe didn't hear the rest. As the silver pendant touched the surface of the nail, a roaring sound filled his ears.

The whole world seemed to tip over. He clung to the rim of the nail with his left hand and gasped for breath.

And spluttered! All at once, there was a pungent smell in the air. Horse dung and smoke. His head whirled. He shut his eyes against the dizziness. It had worked, at last! He'd got himself back into the past again!

But instead of joy, he felt utter panic. For a few moments, he stood there, locked to the spot. He must be crazy! If he hadn't pressed the St. Christopher to the nail, he'd still be in his own time with Dad. Everything would be easy and familiar.

Yet a minute ago, this had been exactly what he wanted. It was like an addiction: it didn't matter how much it scared him, he still came back for more.

He breathed more shallowly, trying to calm down. It was often like this when he arrived in a new world, he reminded himself. It would get better soon. He just had to take it slowly.

With his eyes still closed, he sniffed, deliberately this time. In fact, the smell wasn't nearly as bad as it had been in Jorvik or London. The smoke from the chimneys was as strong as ever, but there wasn't the stink of sewage or rotting food, only a faint smell of drains like on holiday in France. Behind that, he thought he detected something sweet. It made him think of fairgrounds. Candy floss. That couldn't be right!

He opened his eyes, and forgot all about the smell, because the oddest thing was happening. The street was filling up right in front of him. People, carts and horses were emerging from the mist, not moving towards him, but taking shape on the spot. In just a few seconds, the faintest shadows had become solid. The empty street was crowded.

Joe stared. This must have happened before, in London at least, this gathering of figures out of thin air. He guessed he hadn't seen it because he'd been looking at the ground. On impulse, he reached out to touch the cloak of the woman beside him, not quite believing she was real. The cloth felt rough beneath his fingertips, and damp too. The woman glanced his way. Tiny droplets clung to her hair where it had escaped beneath her hood. Her cheeks were flushed with cold. Hurriedly, he drew back his hand. She was as real as him.

Now, voices began to babble around him, as though the volume had just been turned up. The woman was haggling. Other people were chattering, shouting, the street vendors singing and calling their wares. There was a clatter of hooves behind Joe, and a dragging sound. He looked round. The horse was hitched to a kind of sled. In fact, all the things he'd taken for carts were sleds. None of them had wheels.

"Make way! Make way!" The sled-driver eased his horse through the crowd. He seemed not to be in a rush, because his whip hung slack in his hand. He called out again, this time to a man on a ladder, repainting the sign on one of the buildings opposite the Exchange. 'City Printing Office', it said, and beneath that, 'Books Handsomely Bound, Conveniently & Expeditiously Printed', followed by more about handbills, cards, and engraving. Many more people must be able to read in this age, Joe thought. Even so, he recognised the building as Tudor, with its many-paned windows and the upstairs storeys sticking out over the street. The buildings to either side were Tudor too, all with long, wordy signs: a watchmaker, another book binder, and a fire office, whatever that was.

"Young man?" A voice spoke abruptly beside Joe, who jumped. The woman had moved away from the nail, and the man with whom she'd been haggling was now looking expectantly at him. The merchant wore a three-cornered hat rather like a pirate. Presumably, he thought Joe wanted to buy something.

Joe felt his cheeks burn. He stepped back, mumbling an apology. But when he reached the other side of the street and looked up again, the merchant had already found another customer and was spreading things out on the nail for inspection.

Joe looked behind him. He was standing outside

an inn. Like the printer and the watchmaker, this was another Tudor building. He tried to remember what had been opposite the Exchange in his own time. Something old and grand, made of stone, but not as old as this. Beyond the merchant, however, the Exchange and the buildings to either side looked just the same as back in the present. And the café Joe had pointed out was definitely the same building. It seemed to be some kind of coffee house even now, whenever 'now' was.

Men hurried to and fro through the huge oak doors of the Exchange. They looked wealthy in their long, flared coats and white cravats. Almost all of them wore tricorne hats, like the man at the nail. Beneath, they mostly had long hair tied back in a ponytail. Joe peered at a man nearby. His hair must be his own because it wasn't nearly as elaborately styled as William Lucas' wig had been last time.

Joe's heart gave a twitch of excitement. Perhaps one of these merchants might be Lucy's father! If he could find William Lucas, that would lead him to Lucy.

All at once, Joe's mind was filled with memories of her: Lucy with flowers in her hair on her sister's wedding day; a later Lucy, returning at dusk, with wolfhounds at her side; Lucy riding through the woods at Wardour in a long, green dress; and most sharply of all, Lucy's terrified face lit up by the flames of London. The longing to see her again hit him like a

16

punch in the chest. How could he have thought he was ready to forget her?

But of course, even when he found her, she wouldn't remember him. It was always like that. Nobody would know who he was. Yet again, he would have to invent some story to explain himself, and persuade the family to take him in. And then there was the problem of how long he would be able to stay, and the suddenness with which he would disappear again. His worries swarmed up around him.

At that moment, a burst of raucous singing came from down the street.

"Storms that the mast to splinters rend, Can't shake our jovial life!" roared a group of men swaggering up the road. "In ev'ry mess we find a friend, In ev'ry port a wife." The singing grew even louder. "In ev'ry port a wife!" A volley of whistles and whoops followed.

Joe watched, warily. The men were dressed differently to everyone else, in short blue jackets and flat-topped hats. Their pale trousers went down to their shoes, whereas all the other men were wearing knee-length breeches.

Were they sailors, he wondered. But Bristol wasn't on the coast. They looked rough, lawless even, like the men who'd tried to seize him in London. A horrible thought occurred to him. London wasn't near the sea either, but there had been ships there, and he'd very nearly ended up on one of them!

17

Joe shrank back against the wall, trying to make himself invisible. What if these men were on a similar mission, to press-gang others into joining them? His St. Christopher throbbed against his palm, as though trying to draw attention to itself. He clenched his fist around it.

But the sailors shouldered their way into the inn without a glance in Joe's direction. One of them looked African. Joe gazed after him. It was weird to see a black man in historical English costume. In fact, it was weird to see a black man here at all. He looked around the street. Every single person was white. Moreover, they always had been, in every visit to the past, even in London. In fact, the only black face he could remember seeing had been a little slave boy in purple livery in 1666.

When he was sure the sailors weren't coming out again, Joe looked at himself to see where he could put his St. Christopher. Like most of the merchants, he was wearing a long, open overcoat which came down to his calves, brushing his white stockings. Below the stockings, he had shoes with buckles, above them, breeches and another sort of coat, almost as long as the overcoat but cut away at the front. It reminded Joe of the jackets men in his own time sometimes wore to get married. Beneath that, he could see the front of a silk waistcoat. He wondered about putting the St. Christopher in the waistcoat pocket, then decided against it and fastened it round his neck, stuffing it down behind his cravat. It would be safe there until he could give it to Lucy. His worries buzzed up again. What if he didn't find her? But of course he would – somehow.

He put up his hand to rub his forehead. He'd guessed already that he was wearing a hat, a tricorne, to judge by the outline he saw when he rolled his eyes upwards. But his fingertips brushed against something scratchy. The back of his neck was itching, he noticed now. He must be wearing a wig!

He felt around. The wig had a pony tail, and curls at the side, as though it had been put in rollers. Fortunately, his own hair was still there underneath, short and wavy as always. *If I'd known I was coming here, he thought, I could have grown it. That would have been much more comfortable!*

He was just chuckling at the idea when he thought he heard his name.

"Master Joe, sir!"

He turned, then realised his mistake. Whoever it was had to be calling someone else.

But a woman was hurrying towards him. It was clear from her face that she thought she knew him.

Joe glanced around. It had to be him she was looking at. Yet nothing about her was familiar.

In his mind, he ran through all the women he'd met with Lucy. This wasn't her mother, Ellen, nor her Aunt Jane. And she was too old to be either of Lucy's sisters, though of course, they'd been dead in Lucy's last world which almost certainly meant they wouldn't be here.

Was this woman one of the servants then? They would be more likely to call him Master. He cast around in his memory. Perhaps she was Mary. Mary had been in both the last two worlds. But she didn't look anything like her. And she wasn't Mary's daughter, Elizabeth, either.

The next moment, the woman's hand was on his arm. "It *is* you! What good fortune to find you here, Master Josiah! We weren't expecting you till tomorrow. You'll come with me, won't you?"

Joe hesitated. He'd obviously misheard. She had said 'Josiah', not 'Joe, sir'. He ought to correct her straight away.

But already she had taken him by the elbow, and was steering him away through the crowd.

2

"My, but you've grown so tall, Master Josiah!" the woman said, as she led the way along the street. Joe was about to say that his name was actually Joseph, but the woman carried on, "Your mother must be very proud of you! Poor thing, I dare say she's worried sick, having to send you away, with things as they are over there. Anyway, you're safe now. You can write to her as soon as we get back."

Again, Joe opened his mouth to speak. Then he changed his mind. He always had to pretend to be someone else when he arrived in a new time. If this woman thought she knew him, he might as well go along with it, for now at least.

"Is your luggage being sent up from the quay?"

"Yes, Madam," he lied.

"Hark at your lovely manners! But there's no need to call me Madam. Hannah will do, just plain Hannah."

Joe bowed his head to hide his dismay. If the

woman's name was Hannah, he definitely didn't know her. There had never been a Hannah before.

As she shepherded him in and out of all the people, he noticed they were being followed by a pair of small boys, each carrying a collection of boxes and packages. He watched Hannah out of the corner of his eye. Her cloak and bonnet were neat, but she didn't look rich enough to have servants of her own. Did she perhaps run a home for orphans? That might be where she was taking him, though it didn't really make sense. All the same, there was no reason to suppose she was taking him to Lucy's house either.

Joe's stomach churned. Again, he considered excusing himself before he ended up somewhere miles away. But without knowing where he was trying to get to, it was impossible to make a plan.

He might as well try and work out what part of history he'd landed in, he decided, since he'd need to know sooner or later. Of course, the quickest way would be to ask Hannah what year it was. But she would find that very strange. He could only do it if he was sure he was going to walk away once he had his answer. And he wasn't sure. He began looking around for clues instead.

On both sides of the street were quite a few Tudor houses. Some of them looked rather dilapidated, and he saw one along an alley that was actually falling down. The newer buildings, on the other hand, were quite grand. They had flat fronts squared off at the top, and tall windows made from a dozen or so pieces of glass. It occurred to Joe that they were all built of brick or stone. In fact, there were plenty of buildings like this in his own world. Finally, he thought, he'd arrived in an age where things were going to last! No more wooden houses to burn to the ground, which must mean it was after 1666. But how long after?

Dad had said something about eighteenth century merchants at the Exchange, and the man at the nail had been doing exactly what Dad had described. So maybe this *was* the eighteenth century. That seemed reasonable, and Joe felt extra pleased with himself for remembering that the eighteenth century was the 1700s, not the 1800s. He was so much better at historical detective work than his school friends would be!

When he tried to recall anything at all about the eighteenth century, however, his satisfaction drained away. At some point, there had been some kings called George, one of whom had gone mad. But he had no idea when that had been, except that it was sometime after Elizabeth I. If it was now, that would make this Georgian England. But even if that was right, it meant nothing to him.

Hannah had paused at a vegetable barrow and was haggling for five cabbages and half a sack of carrots. She must have a lot of people to feed, Joe thought. She turned to the boys and beckoned the second one, who dumped the packages he was carrying in the arms of the first and took the crate of vegetables, balancing it on his head.

"Mind you bring the box back," growled the vegetable seller.

Hannah paid the man. "Here's an extra farthing for the boy when he does," she said.

The man grunted and put the coin in his apron with the rest of the money. Joe wondered if the boy would get it.

"That's everything now," Hannah said to Joe. She sounded apologetic. "The carriage is just beyond St. Leonard's Gate." She nodded towards the junction ahead of them. "The thing is, you can't bring wheeled vehicles into the old part of the city."

"Why not?" Joe asked.

"The cellars are just beneath the streets. A cart could go straight through the road. That's why the merchants use sleds. But it's not far to walk," she added hastily.

The mist seemed to be thickening. Joe kept close to Hannah. Having decided to stay with her, he didn't want to lose her by accident.

There was a different smell now that hadn't been there before, a muddy, watery smell, as though the river was close by. Joe squinted into the fog, but couldn't see anything much. Bristol did have a waterfront – he and Dad had walked along it yesterday evening – but that should have been some distance from here.

"There we are," Hannah said.

The outline of two horses appeared, waiting patiently side by side. An open carriage was hitched to them. It had two benches but no roof over it, more like a smart sort of cart than a luxury vehicle.

The first boy stacked his boxes and packets carefully beneath one of the benches. But the second tipped his cabbages and carrots straight onto the floor of the carriage, and dashed off, back through the gates.

Hannah muttered something, then gave a farthing to the first boy, who tested it between his teeth before hurrying away. "They could learn some manners from you, Master Josiah," she grumbled, sweeping the vegetables under the bench and gesturing for Joe to climb into the carriage beside her. "You remember Samuel?"

A boy older than Joe sat on the driver's seat, holding the reins. He lifted his hat to Joe and nodded. Joe did the same. He didn't think he'd ever seen Samuel before. But Samuel seemed to know him.

Joe rested his hand on the side of the carriage. He was almost sure this was one of Lucy's worlds. Every other time his St. Christopher had taken him into the past, she had been there, even if it had taken him a while to find her. After all, hadn't he gone with someone he hadn't recognised last time, who'd turned out to be her father?

Except that that had been different! If William Lucas had introduced himself, Joe would have known it would be alright. This time, he was certain he didn't know either Hannah or Samuel. The fact that they thought they knew him didn't change that. If anything, it made it more wrong, not less! Nobody should know him here.

He cleared his throat. "I should probably just, er, check whether …" He broke off, at a loss for how to finish. If he was going to abandon Hannah, it hardly mattered what he said.

She waited, her head on one side, then glanced past him. "Oh good, here's Mary," she said.

Joe looked round. Another woman in a cloak and bonnet was approaching, followed by another small boy. Joe caught his breath. He did know this woman! This was unquestionably the lady's maid from Wardour who'd worked for Lucy's family in London too. Even her name was right. So it was going to be okay after all!

Before he could greet her, however, Hannah said, "Master Josiah, this is Mrs Mary Stanton, our housekeeper. She's new to the household since you were last here. Mary, this is Master Josiah de Courson, arrived early."

Mary curtsied. Joe bowed. "It's a pleasure to make your acquaintance, Madam," he said, offering his hand to help her up into the carriage. She took it, her expression politely pleasant but nothing more.

Joe was bewildered. He was sure this was the Mary he knew, so it must be alright to go with her and

Hannah. But it didn't make sense – Hannah and Samuel thought they knew him, even though he didn't know them; and the person he did recognise didn't know him at all.

Mary's boxes were stowed and the boy dismissed.

"You wanted to check something, Master Josiah?" Hannah said.

"No, it's fine." Joe climbed up to sit next to Mary. The horses began to move forward.

He looked around, more relaxed now. The road was busy with people, horses, carts and sleds. Joe blinked. Behind a church to his left, he thought he'd glimpsed the rigging of a sailing ship. He must be imagining things.

But a little further on, the street broadened and the carriage did indeed emerge onto a quay. Moored all the way along the wharves were sailing boats of all sizes including a towering ship, its furled sails pale in the blank sky. Gulls wheeled round in the fog, screeching, and one perched on the prow of the ship, beady eyes alert.

Joe looked along the quay. A man staggered out of a nearby warehouse with a huge sack on his shoulder, followed by two more men rolling barrels. Porters hurried to and fro, while an official with a list oversaw the hoisting of wooden crates over the side of the big ship using a kind of crane attached to a hut. Two merchants were quarrelling over the weight of something, and Joe saw money change hands surreptitiously between two others. Meanwhile, sailors swarmed over many of the vessels, cleaning, mending and adjusting all manner of things that Joe couldn't name.

Samuel guided the carriage across a bridge. The water beneath was sluggish. Joe remembered the Thames at the time of the Great Fire. The river here looked just as murky and disgusting, even if the streets were cleaner.

On the other side, Samuel turned the horses back along the quay. It was less busy here, but the buildings crowded down to the water, making the wharf narrow.

As the carriage moved slowly along, Joe tried to get his bearings from what he remembered of the modern city. But it was impossible! He couldn't work out at all where the glassy waterfront would one day rise up, and though he saw one short row of houses that might have been there in his own time, he couldn't be sure. In his world, cars would be pouring past, not the river.

They passed another church and came to a triangular green studded with trees. Along one side was a third church, this one very large. Joe peered through the mist. He was sure he and Dad had driven past an open space like this yesterday evening. The big church looked like Bristol Cathedral except that part of it was missing. He was baffled. Usually, buildings were whole in the past, even when they were ruins in the present. How could only some of the cathedral be there? It was as though it was only half-grown.

"I expect you remember this from before, Master Josiah," Hannah said.

Joe thought it best to nod.

"The Backs and College Green probably haven't altered much," she went on. "But Park Street is changing from month to month."

Joe leaned out to look. At the corner of the green, the carriage speeded up slightly as it went down into a dip, then the horses slowed to a crawl as the road climbed up a very steep hill. There were just a few houses on either side of the street, all with railings at the front; then a row which seemed to be half finished; and then trees and open country beyond. It looked as though they were on the edge of the city already. He wondered how far they were going to travel.

But Samuel drew the horses to a stop and climbed down.

"We're here?" Joe was taken aback. It didn't seem worth taking the carriage for such a short trip, even for Hannah and Mary's shopping.

"I told you Park Street is changing!" Hannah said. "Those houses up there have come on quite a bit in the last two years, haven't they? It changes the feel of the street. And you see the scaffolds further up? It'll be a long road when it's finished." She waved a hand. "Houses are going up all over this side of Bristol, and on Clifton Hill as well."

They all climbed down from the carriage. Two girls had come up the steps from the basement of the house and began unloading the packages. Mary followed them down. Joe was about to go with her.

"Not the servants' entrance for you!" scolded Hannah. She led the way up a set of stone steps to the front door, and pulled the bell-pull.

Almost immediately, the door was opened by a man in livery and a white wig.

"Master Josiah de Courson," announced Hannah. "I met him by chance in the city. His ship must have come in earlier than expected." To Joe, she said, "You remember Morley, our butler?"

"Of course!" Joe grinned. How funny, he thought! This was the steward from Old Wardour, but he looked so different in a wig.

"Welcome, Master Josiah." Morley bowed, unsmiling. Joe's grin fell from his face. He stepped meekly inside. Behind him, Hannah went back down the steps and through the gate in the railings.

Morley closed the front door. "I'll tell the Mistress you're here."

"Thank you."

Joe looked about him. He was standing in a wide hallway with a broad flight of stairs at the end and doors to either side. He took off his coat and hat, and patted his wig, hoping it was still on straight.

Now that he was actually here, in Lucy's house,

he felt sick with nerves. At least he'd made it to the right place, he reminded himself. He wouldn't even have to explain who he was, since her mother would know, or would think she did. And there was no doubt that he would be allowed to stay.

But in exchange for that, he was going to have to pretend to be someone he'd never met, about whom he knew absolutely nothing.

"Josiah de Courson," he repeated under his breath. Who on earth was he? Did Lucy know him? She must do, if he'd been here two years ago. Would she and her mother make the same mistake as Hannah? Or would they see through Joe straight away? He swallowed.

Even worse, there would surely come a moment when the real Josiah de Courson arrived. What would happen then?

But there was no time to think about it. Morley was gesturing to take Joe's coat and hat. He ushered Joe forward. With a hammering heart, Joe stepped into Lucy's new life.

3

But Lucy wasn't in the room he entered. Instead, her mother rose to greet him.

"Josiah! This is an unexpected pleasure!" She wore a grey silk dress with a high waist and a swathe of material at the bosom. Her mouth was turned up in a smile that didn't reach her eyes.

The room itself was not very large, but it was elegant and light, with a high ceiling and a tall window that overlooked the street. Two chairs were drawn up either side of the fire. Between them was a prim sofa in pink silk with a curvy back, like a huge mouth waiting to eat him, Joe thought. Above the mantelpiece was a circular mirror that made the room appear to bulge.

"Madam." Joe stopped in front of Ellen and bowed, disconcerted that she didn't seem very happy to see him.

"Aunt Ellen, please," she corrected him. "We can't be too formal. You may be staying for a long time." She motioned to him to sit down. "I'm sorry we weren't there to meet you. My sister wrote that we should expect you tomorrow or the day after, depending on the weather. Did you have a good crossing?"

"Yes, thank you." Joe's brain was whirring. Hannah had mentioned a ship, and Josiah's surname sounded French. He must be coming across the English Channel.

"Morley tells me that our cook happened to see you down in the city. Your luggage is to follow, I assume?"

"That's right," Joe agreed.

"And how *are* you?" A sympathetic note crept into Ellen's voice. "I know my sister will be glad to have you safe in England. I wrote to her that she and your father are most welcome to join you here at any time. Your father still believes it won't be necessary. I pray he's right." She bit her lip, then said quickly, "Of course, there's no need for you to worry. Everything will turn out for the best, I'm sure."

Joe tried to adopt a suitable expression, without quite knowing what it should be. It sounded as though Josiah's family was in trouble of some kind.

Just then, the door opened.

"Ah, here's your cousin!" Lucy's mother was plainly relieved to change the subject.

The girl who crossed the room towards Joe wore a long blue gown drawn in at the waist with a ribbon.

Her hair tumbled over her shoulders in a dark mass, neither pinned up nor covered by any kind of cap.

Joe watched the graceful way she moved. Then the familiar blue eyes caught his gaze. Something flipped over inside him.

He stood up.

"Lucy!" It should have been an exclamation of delight, but it came out as a croak. His mouth seemed to have turned to wood, and his arms felt rigid, even though his chest swelled with happiness at seeing her again.

"Cousin Josiah," Lucy replied coolly. "How do you do?" She curtseyed.

Joe's chest shrank a little. She didn't sound very friendly.

He cleared his throat. "I'm well, thank you." He didn't sound terribly friendly either, he realised. Were they both suffering from the same horrible shyness? He felt as though he'd been frozen to the spot.

Yet there was nothing shy about Lucy's manner. Had she perhaps realised immediately that he wasn't Josiah? But there was no sign of that either.

Joe floundered. If Lucy believed him to be her cousin, and she wasn't shy, why was she so offhand?

"Are you well yourself?" he asked, bending himself to bow.

"I am, thank you." She raised her eyebrows. "Your English has improved. You don't have an accent at all now. Have you been in the country long?"

34

For a moment, Joe was confused. "I've only just arrived," he said. Then he realised what she meant. Presumably, he should have had a French accent, but it was too late to put one on now.

"How are your parents and brothers?" Lucy asked.

"They're well, thank you," Joe said. He waited to see if she would reveal anything about them.

"My brother will be sorry that Henry isn't with you," she said. "Is he still studying in Paris? Or is it too dangerous now?"

Lucy's mother shot her a look. "Shall we have some tea?" she interrupted.

"Now?" There was no mistaking Lucy's surprise.

"Why not?" Ellen forced a smile. "It's not every day that we have an occasion such as this. Why don't you both sit down?" She picked up a small bell from a table beside her chair and rang it.

At once, a footman in livery appeared. He must have been standing right outside the door.

"Bring us the tea things please, Jackson," Ellen said. "And perhaps something to eat?" She looked at Joe. "I expect you breakfasted early on the ship. Are you hungry?"

Joe was suddenly aware of the cavernous feeling in his stomach. How had he managed to forget how starving he'd been? It must be over an hour since he'd left Dad. "Yes, I am," he replied enthusiastically.

"Ask Hannah to send up some luncheon as well

then please, Jackson," Lucy's mother said curtly. "You may remember, Josiah, we eat earlier in this household than more fashionable houses. We have breakfast soon after eight, rather than ten, and dinner at two instead of four."

Joe nodded, hoping his puzzlement didn't show. Breakfast he could understand, but if Hannah was going to provide lunch now, in the middle of the morning, did that mean dinner was the evening meal? And if so, was it at two in the afternoon, which would be weirdly early for the evening, or two in the morning, which would be ridiculously late?

"Your uncle likes a good meal when he returns from the sugar house," Ellen was saying. "We're so used to the routine that we keep to it even though he's away."

"Has he been gone long?" Joe asked cautiously. He knew this was risky. Josiah might be expected to know the answer already. But equally, if he wasn't, it would seem odd *not* to ask.

"He's out in the West Indies," Ellen said. "His brother James, Lucy's uncle, died last summer. James had lived out there for years with his wife and son. Truth be told, we're rather afraid of the state of his plantation. He was a very different man to my husband." She checked herself. "In any case, his widow wrote to William, begging him to come and help settle James' affairs. Her letter arrived in October and he sailed the same week."

"But that's four months ago," Joe said. As soon as he'd spoken, he was afraid he'd made a mistake. Was it February here, like it was at home?

But Ellen only nodded. "The voyage can take as long as two months, you know," she said. "Even if he'd turned for home the day he arrived in Jamaica, he'd scarcely be back by now. And how long it will take for him to make the necessary arrangements, we simply don't know."

"So it's just the two of you and Peter in the house, besides the servants?" Joe ventured. This was really dangerous ground, but it was worth taking a chance to find out.

"And Thomas," Ellen said. "Did you not know I had another child? He's upstairs with his nurse."

"Is he ill?" Joe asked without thinking.

"No. At least, not as far as I know. Why do you ask?" Lucy's mother frowned.

Joe blushed and shook his head. It was a silly thing to have said. The word 'nurse' used to mean something like 'nanny', he remembered now. But his brain had connected the modern meaning with the memory of Lucy's baby brother dying during the Plague in her last world.

He studied his hands, embarrassed and perplexed. Hadn't that baby been called Thomas too? Was this the same boy? Surely it couldn't be. Lucy's older brother, Matthew, had died when she lived in Tudor times, and he'd still been dead when Joe met her again in London. Similarly, her sisters, Anne and Cecily, had died in Lucy's last life. They didn't seem to be here, nor did he expect to see them, any more than he expected to see her long-dead brother Francis. So how could the baby be alive again?

When Joe looked up, there was a tightness in Ellen's expression. An awkward silence fell, broken only when the footman entered the room.

He set the tray he was carrying down beside Ellen. On it were three cups with saucers, two silver pots, a bowl of something white, and a plate of dainty little sandwiches. Even if he ate them all, Joe knew he would still be hungry. So luncheon must just be a snack, and dinner must be what he would think of as lunch.

Lucy rose and took a small key from her mother, went to the bureau, unlocked it, and brought back a polished wooden box. Ellen produced a second key and unlocked the box. What could be in there, Joe wondered, that was so precious?

Inside were two compartments with a glass bowl in between. Lucy's mother opened both and spooned something dark and dry from each one into the bowl. She stirred, breathed in the fragrance, then added another spoonful before emptying the bowl into one of the silver pots and adding hot water from the other through a tiny tap.

This must be the tea, Joe realised. He had no idea tea had ever been so valuable or the process for making it so careful. Ellen locked the box again and gave it to Lucy to put away.

Joe looked at the tray. Was the bowl of white stuff sugar? It didn't look much like it. The pieces were sharp, uneven shards, as though a larger block had been broken up quite roughly. All the same, he couldn't think what else it could be.

Ellen added a spoonful to each cup and handed one to Joe. He took a sip, slightly hesitantly. He didn't usually didn't drink tea at home, but this tasted more or less like he expected, and it was sweet, too.

Lucy's mother now picked up the sandwich platter and handed it to Joe with a plate and fork. Again, Joe was surprised. But this time, he had to hide a smile. He'd become quite the historian, he thought, because it wasn't the idea of eating sandwiches with a fork that had struck him as unusual. It was the fact that there *were* forks. There had never been forks in the past! There hadn't been tea or sandwiches either, of course. Really, this place felt altogether much more familiar than Lucy's earlier times.

As he was finishing the sandwiches he had taken, the clock in the hall chimed very loudly. Joe counted. Ten o'clock.

"Lucy needs to return to her studies," Ellen said, suddenly brisk. "Would you like to rest, Josiah? Morley can show you to your room. Or you can go with your cousin to her lessons, if you wish. I'm sure Miss Waters won't mind."

"I'll go with Lucy," Joe answered swiftly. The chiming clock had reminded him that he didn't know how long he would be here. He should make the most of every second.

Lucy stood up. "Very well," she said. Joe thought he saw her grimace. He bowed to Ellen, then followed Lucy out of the room.

"Who is your teacher?" he asked, as they went down the hall.

"I have a governess." Lucy didn't look at him as she spoke. "She gives me lessons every day except Sunday."

She led the way up the stairs to the first floor landing. A door stood open ahead of them. It seemed to be the dining room.

"Do you eat meals up here?" he asked.

"Of course! Don't you remember?"

"Not very well, I'm afraid," he said. "How long were we here? I don't recall."

"Over a month," Lucy said tersely. "Long enough!"

Joe winced, partly at his apparent lack of memory of such a long stay, but mostly at her tone. Lucy had been angry with him in the past, generally when she'd found out he had lied to her about who he really was. But underneath it all, he'd still felt sure she liked him. This time, he was pretty sure she didn't.

She continued up another flight of stairs to the second floor, not troubling to point out what any of the rooms were. "In here," she said, pushing open one of the doors.

The room was small but light, and looked out over the garden. A young woman sat on a bed reading. She stood up quickly and closed the book. Her dark hair was wound up at the back of her head and she wore a long, dark dress. She looked vaguely familiar, Joe thought.

"You're back, Miss Lucy!" she said. "I thought perhaps we'd finished for the day."

Joe closed his eyes for a second. He knew this voice, he was sure. He searched around in his memory for someone from Lucy's worlds with a name like Waters. But there wasn't anyone.

"This is my cousin, Josiah de Courson," Lucy was saying. "My mother's sister married a French Count, you may remember. Josiah's staying for a while until things settle down over there."

Miss Waters gave a little curtsey. "Enchantée, Maître Josiah. Vous êtes très bienvenu pour nous rejoindre."

Panic rose inside Joe. He'd started French at school last year, but he wasn't up to any sort of conversation, never mind trying to pass himself off as French.

"I'm very pleased to meet you, Miss Waters," he said determinedly in English.

"Goodness! What perfect pronunciation!" Miss Waters exclaimed. "But of course, your mother must have taught you." She turned back to Lucy. "Is Master Josiah to be schooled with you, Miss Lucy, not Master Peter?"

"Peter's school isn't expecting him until next week."

"So he'll join our lessons for the next few days?"

"If he wishes." It was perfectly clear from Lucy's voice that she didn't.

"Let's begin our reading lesson, then. Perhaps you would like to draw up that chair from the corner, Master Josiah." Miss Waters pointed to a stubby armchair like the ones downstairs. It looked more comfortable than the wooden seats she and Lucy were sitting on. Joe did as he was told, waiting for Lucy to scowl at him again. But she ignored him and pulled a huge leather-bound Bible towards her.

She began to read from where Miss Waters indicated, running her finger along the page. Joe listened to her stumbling over words that weren't especially difficult. Then came a section which she read faultlessly, as though she knew it off by heart. He paid closer attention. The language was older and more poetic than the Bible they used at his school, but these were the Ten Commandments. That was why she knew it!

After that, she read on, hesitantly again, before breaking off altogether. "Shouldn't Josiah read some?"

"Very well." The governess pushed the Bible across the desk towards Joe. "Exodus, chapter 21, verse 15."

Joe gulped. He wasn't used to finding the verses like this. He scanned the page until he spotted the number 15, and began.

" 'And he that -' " He paused. The next word was 'fmiteth'. He glanced through the text. There were lots of 'f's but hardly any of them made sense.

"Smiteth," prompted Miss Waters.

"Right. 'He that smiteth his father, or his mother -' " Joe stopped again. Here were two more. This wasn't as easy as he'd thought.

"Shall be surely …" read Miss Waters.

"Oh, the 'f's are actually 's's! 'Shall be surely put to death. And he that' … er … 'stealeth a man and felleth' – no – 'selleth him, or if he be found …' Should that be sound?"

"No, found."

" 'He that stealeth a man and selleth him, or if he be found in his hand, he … shall surely be put to death'."

Miss Waters nodded. "Continue."

For some time, Joe read on. It was tricky, spotting the 'f's before he misread them, but he got better at it. Soon he was reading a good deal more fluently than Lucy.

"Very good," Miss Waters said, as he came to the end of the chapter. "I think Miss Lucy should read on from here." Lucy glared.

For the next hour or so, they took it in turns to

read. Joe read better and better, and looked forward to his turn because it gave him something to do. Listening to Lucy struggle was frustrating and dull.

At last, Miss Waters said, "That's enough for today. I've been thinking, perhaps we should make the most of the fact that we have Master Josiah with us."

Lucy glowered, but Joe looked up with interest. Perhaps the governess was about to suggest something more fun.

"Why don't we vary our usual routine?" Miss Waters went on. "Instead of working on your writing next, I propose we continue with French. It will be much better for you to practise with Master Josiah than with me, Miss Lucy. Shall we do that?"

4

Joe's heart stopped for a second, then beat twice as fast.

"That wouldn't be fair on Lucy," he said quickly. His mouth was dry. "Speaking a language as your mother tongue is quite different from having to learn it." He realised as he said this that French wasn't actually Josiah's mother tongue.

He pressed on. "I don't know that I'd be able to help her. And I'm not sure she'd want me to." He didn't look at Lucy, but he was sure she wouldn't contradict him. "I think we should carry on with the writing lesson, as you normally would."

"Are you quite sure?" Miss Waters sounded disappointed.

Joe nodded vigorously. Out of the corner of his eye, he saw Lucy staring at him in disbelief.

"Very well, as you wish."

The governess pulled a wooden tray across the desk towards her on which were three small glass pots.

One was filled with something white and had lots of holes in the lid like a pepper shaker; another had four larger holes in the lid, two of them with broken feathers sticking out of them; and the third had a lid with no holes and something black inside. Miss Waters opened this last pot.

"Have you another quill for Master Josiah?" she asked Lucy.

Lucy opened a drawer in the desk and brought out a feather. She handed it to Joe with a knife and a wooden board. They seemed to be expecting him to cut his own pen.

Joe placed the feather across the board, and sliced the blunt end off it. Then he cut a bit more off one side. He inspected it. If this were a fountain pen, it would have a short slit down to the tip. He cut one in the longer side, then took the quill in his hand and looked up, hoping very much that he'd got it roughly right.

For a moment, there was absolute silence.

Then Miss Waters said, "Perhaps Miss Lucy could show you how it's done."

Without speaking, Lucy took the feather from Joe. In a series of deft moves, she cut a large section from the back of the shaft, hooked something out from inside, cut curves either side of the nib, slit it, scraped it, and trimmed it to length, then broke off the upper part of the feather.

"I suppose you have someone to do this for you

at home," she said scornfully, handing him the finished quill.

Joe looked at it. Whichever way he answered would be wrong. "Thank you, Lucy," he said quietly.

A flicker of confusion passed across her face, but she didn't reply.

Miss Waters pushed a sheet of paper towards each of them. Joe imitated Lucy, shaking white powder from the first pot onto the paper. He'd always thought this was done afterwards to dry the ink, but it seemed not. They brushed the powder into the surface of the paper, then tipped what was left back into a dish.

Miss Waters took up the Bible once more and began to read slowly aloud. Writing must mean dictation, Joe guessed. He followed Lucy's example, dipping his quill in the ink pot. Before the tip touched the paper, however, a large black drop splashed right across the middle. Lucy's head was down but Joe could feel her disdain radiating across the desk.

As he began to scratch out the first few letters, a cloud of fine drops sprayed out. Pointedly, Lucy moved her paper away from him.

When it happened a second time, she hissed, "Ruin your own work by all means, but don't ruin mine!"

"I'm sorry," Joe mumbled. "I'm no good at this."

"You've noticed!" she retorted. But her voice was less sharp than before.

47

The next hour felt like an eternity. It wasn't difficult to make marks on the paper with the quill, not like it had been scraping letters into wax in Roman times. But Joe's pen left a trail of black spots every time he dipped it in the inkwell, and he only seemed to manage one or two awkward letters before he needed to dip it again. Miss Waters had to read every sentence twice or three times before Joe had got it down. Lucy, on the other hand, wrote each line smoothly, and then sighed loudly while she waited for Joe to catch up.

By the end of the lesson, the page in front of Joe looked as though a dozen spiders had swum in the ink and then danced themselves to death across the paper. He could hardly bear to look at Miss Waters as he handed it over.

She pinched her lips together. "I see there is work to be done, Master Josiah," she said drily. "The Master at the grammar school will not be impressed by this."

Joe hung his head.

"I shall give you the benefit of the doubt and say that the pen Miss Lucy cut for you didn't suit your hand." She held up a finger to silence Lucy's immediate protest. "Of course, that is all the more reason to learn to cut your own quills."

Joe nodded mutely.

Miss Waters looked at Lucy's work. "There are errors here, here, and here, Miss Lucy. And you've entirely missed the sense of this part here."

"But it's much better than Cousin Josiah's!" Lucy cried.

"Clearly. But Master Josiah read much better than you. Now," Miss Waters went on, "we would usually do painting next. But after this last disastrous hour, I hesitate to embark on something Master Josiah won't have learned." She turned to Joe. "Are you quite sure you wouldn't prefer to do French instead?"

"No, really, let's do painting!" Joe said desperately. "I have done some. Actually, I've had more practice with a paintbrush than a quill."

The dumbfounded expressions on the others' faces told Joe he shouldn't have said this. He hurried on. "We do things differently where I come from. If you don't mind me having a go, I'm willing to try."

Miss Waters shrugged. "In that case, let's go down to the library. We've been painting in there while the master's away from home." She swept them before her out of the room.

Lucy was preoccupied as they went down the stairs. Joe wondered if she'd now guessed that he wasn't Josiah. He thought about telling her the truth. The trouble was, she would find it hard to believe. She always did. On the other hand, at least she was unlikely to be angry with him this time. All the same, this wasn't an ideal moment, with Miss Waters at their heels.

On the ground floor, Lucy opened the door diagonally opposite the room where they'd had tea earlier. This room was slightly larger, and like Miss Waters' room it looked out over the garden behind the house. Joe surveyed the glass-fronted bookcase which took up most of one wall. There had hardly been any books in Lucy's worlds before. Even last time, there had only been a dozen or so in the whole house. Here, there must be several hundred.

"My father is very proud of his library," Lucy said, following Joe's gaze.

"It's impressive," Joe said. "Where I come from –" He stopped.

"Where you come from, what?" There was an edge to Lucy's tone.

"I was just thinking, a library like this would be incredibly valuable."

"I suppose it probably is," Lucy said in surprise. "But you live in a castle, don't you? I'm sure your father's library is twice the size!"

Joe wondered whether Josiah was in the habit of showing off to his English cousins. That must be very annoying.

He looked around the rest of the room. Beneath the window stood a large leather-topped desk with a chair. This must also be William's study as well as the library, Joe realised. At each end of the desk was a globe on a wooden stand. One seemed to show countries, but the other had strange patterns of lines and dots on it.

"That's a celestial globe," Lucy said, "though I

don't learn astronomy." She watched him warily, waiting for his reply.

"Nor do I," Joe said with a shrug. He was pleased to see her almost smile.

Two chairs had been pushed back to the wall on either side of the fireplace and a pair of easels stood in the middle of the room.

Miss Waters went to the mantelpiece, and pulled a knob beside it. A few moments later, a maid appeared. "Could you fetch Miss Anne's easel and palette for Master Josiah?" Miss Waters asked her. "If there are brushes, bring those too, and three pots of water."

While they waited for the maid to return, Miss Waters lit a taper from the fire that burned in the grate, and carried it over to a wall bracket where she lit four tall candles. Their light fell on the paintings already on the easels. Both were of the same landscape, but the one on the left was a good deal better than the one on the right.

Lucy's governess walked around the room, looking at the pictures on the walls. "Which shall we attempt today?" she asked Lucy.

"Couldn't we do one of the portraits? I've always liked the picture of the lady in the hat outside the dining room."

"That will have to wait until we progress to oils," Miss Waters answered. "How about this one?" She took a painting off the wall and propped it on a chair. How odd, Joe thought, to paint from a painting. But of course, cameras wouldn't have been invented yet, so Lucy couldn't paint from a photograph. And unless they went out specially, she couldn't paint a real landscape either.

As though she'd heard his thought, Lucy said, "Miss Waters and I are going out to the Avon Gorge in the summer, to paint the ships coming up to Bristol." Her face was bright. Then uncertainty flickered across it. "Although ships are very fiddly, and of course, they'll be moving, too. I have to get better first."

Joe smiled. She sounded suddenly much more like the old Lucy.

The third easel was set up, and Miss Waters gave Lucy and Joe paper, brushes, and palettes on which to mix their paints. This was like at school, Joe thought. Proper artists' materials, not kids' paints.

He began putting washes across the paper just as Miss Waters did at her own easel. He'd learnt about watercolours last term, so he managed every bit as well as Lucy. When eventually he stood back and looked at his finished picture, he was quite proud of the result.

"It's very good!" Miss Waters said, failing to hide her amazement. "Do boys usually learn to paint in France?"

"Not always," Joe said carefully. "But I like to draw, so my mother taught me to paint." Part of this was true at least – he had got into drawing in the last couple of years – so it was better than an outright lie.

He looked at Lucy's painting. It was just as good as his, yet Miss Waters hadn't commented on it at all.

"I like the way you've done those trees," he said. "They've turned out better than mine."

Lucy lowered her eyes. "Thank you," she said shyly.

"Go and wash your hands ready for dinner, then," Miss Waters said.

Once again, Joe realised how hungry he was. He'd been so absorbed in painting, he hadn't noticed the time. In the hall, the grandfather clock showed almost two o'clock.

Lucy led the way into a small room beside the front door. "You're different to how you were before," she said abruptly.

Joe swallowed. "How was I before?"

She looked away, as though she hadn't meant to start this conversation. "I don't know. More French maybe, at least you sounded more French. But also…" She paused. "Not as nice, especially not to me. You used to make fun of me all the time. I thought you didn't like me. And you were always boasting about everything."

Joe thought quickly. "Maybe I've grown up a bit," he said. "I do like you a lot. I'm really happy to see you again." At once, his cheeks blazed. Why had he said that? It was true, but he needn't have told her!

Lucy's cheeks turned pink too.

Joe looked around for a way of changing the subject. There was another mirror in this room, a normal one this time, and a delicate table beneath it with a round pot and two silver containers like larger versions of the shaker on the inkstand.

"What's in those?" he asked, pointing.

"Powder," Lucy said.

"What for?"

"For my parents and their visitors to powder their wigs before they go out." She looked at him quizzically. "This is the powder room after all."

Joe looked as his feet. Presumably, he should have known that.

Lucy went to the corner of the room where there was a washstand. On it was a bowl, a small dish with a piece of white soap, and a matching jug. She poured water into the bowl and washed her hands, then waited for Joe to do the same. Joe was glad to see that the water looked clean. In Lucy's house in London, water had come through pipes to a tap over the kitchen sink, but it had been yellow and foul.

"Do you need –?" She opened a door Joe hadn't noticed because it was wallpapered to match the rest of the room. Behind it was a space that was barely more than a cupboard, with a thigh-high wooden box from which came the most revolting smell.

"It's a water closet," Lucy said, thinking Joe didn't understand. "The very latest design."

Joe knew from experience that he must be

looking at a toilet. And of course, the initials of 'water closet' were still used in his own world to mean loo. But what did the box have to do with water? There was no sign of any plumbing.

Lucy stepped forward and lifted the lid. The stench was even worse. Joe shut his mouth tight and tried not to breathe.

A large bowl painted with flowers had been set into a wooden seat. The bowl had a big hole in the bottom and a smaller hole in the side. Mounted on the seat was a handle, and next to it, half a book, its pages torn off. "When you've finished," Lucy explained, "you pull the handle, and water pours in through that hole and washes everything out through the bottom."

"Right." Joe was still mystified. The water must come from a tank inside the box, but where did the poo get flushed to? As far as he could see, it must end up in the box as well, underneath the bowl. So it was really just a glorified potty. No wonder it stank!

"You notice the closet bowl matches the washing bowl and the jug?" Lucy continued. "The porcelain is by Mr. Wedgwood!"

Joe could tell from the way she spoke that he was supposed to be impressed. He did his best.

Content, Lucy led the way back upstairs again to the dining room. This room was much bigger than either the library or the parlour, with two windows looking out over the street. It was really light in here, Joe thought, lighter than it had ever been indoors in the past. A fire burned in this grate too. Every room would have a fire, of course. Even Miss Waters' room had had one.

The dining table was laid with silver cutlery on a white cloth. At each place, there was a china plate, a wine glass, and a small bowl and slightly taller pot both made of blue glass. Five people were expected to eat, it seemed. The servants must be eating below stairs.

Ellen entered the room and sat down at the head of the table. Lucy sat down to her mother's left, and motioned to Joe to take the seat beside her.

"How did you get on this morning?" Ellen asked.

"Quite well," Lucy said. "Cousin Josiah is very good at painting." Joe waited for her to add that he was really terrible at writing, but she didn't.

"How unusual," Ellen said. "Have you been schooled in other arts as well? Do you play the pianoforte?"

"No, Madam - I mean, Aunt." Joe coloured.

"If you'd like to learn, you could join Lucy for her lessons while you're here. But perhaps that would be odd." Ellen seemed to change her mind. "After all, it will be of little use to you later."

Joe didn't reply. In actual fact, he did have piano lessons at home, but he couldn't bear to be asked to play. He wondered why Ellen might consider it useful for Lucy to learn the piano but not him.

Silence fell as they waited for the other two chairs to be filled. Joe assumed that her brother, Peter, was going to sit in one of them. He must be on his way home from school now. But that still left an extra seat.

Joe was aware of worry buzzing inside him again as he contemplated this. There had been extra chairs around the table in Lucy's last world, several of them for her dead brothers and sisters. But it couldn't be that here.

Suddenly, the worry tightened into a knot of cold, hard dread. How could he have forgotten? In London, there had been another person at the table, Joe's arch enemy, the boy who had tried several times to kill him. Nobody had mentioned him yet, but Lucy's world wouldn't be complete without him. He was bound to be here somewhere!

Joe watched the doorway with mounting panic. Surely, the missing person was Tobias.

5

It was Miss Waters who sat down opposite Joe, however. She was followed into the room by a boy Joe recognised at once as Peter, rubbing his hands, his cheeks rosy.

"I'm so hungry, I could eat a horse!" he declared.

"That won't be necessary," Ellen replied tersely. "You remember your cousin, Josiah?"

Peter's grin faded. He bowed to Joe.

"As you know, he'll be staying with us for the next few months."

Peter nodded. "We hear things are heating up over there," he said to Joe. "Did your king really try to flee? They're saying he's not fit to rule any more! Is there actually going to be a revolution?" He sounded gleeful.

"Peter!" Ellen rebuked him. "Have a little tact!"

"Sorry," Peter said, in a voice that wasn't at all sorry. "I was only wondering if the rumours were true."

"I don't know," Joe said honestly. He tried to look worried, but he was barely listening to Peter. All he could think about was that Tobias didn't seem to be here after all. The prospect of being in Lucy's world without him was enough to make Joe want to cheer!

He made an effort to put the older boy out of his mind and focus on what Peter was saying. It sounded like Lucy's brother was talking about the French Revolution. Joe didn't know much about it, except that they'd used a frame with a blade that fell on a person's neck and cut their head off. He couldn't remember what it was called, but he did remember that it had been the rich who'd been executed, earls and counts and so on.

All at once, everything clicked into place. *My mother's sister married a French Count,* Lucy had said. So that was why Josiah had been sent away, and why Ellen had suggested his parents come too. They were in danger of being executed! Joe felt a flush of satisfaction at solving the puzzle. He tried not to let it show.

"Shall we say Grace?" Lucy's mother said, pointedly.

"Now, Josiah," she went on afterwards, "let me explain what all the food is." She gestured to the dishes the footmen were bringing to the table from a shelf behind a door in the corner of the room. Joe couldn't work out how so much food came from such a small space, until he saw the shelf disappear downwards and come back up again refilled. It must be some sort of lift.

"The soup to start is hare," Ellen said. "Then there's beef steak pie, those are potted pigeons, that's apple pie coming now, and a calf's foot jelly. This one is crimped haddocks, and over there is a saddle of mutton. There's also blancmange, and that's a roasted turkey, of course. After the soup, it's service à la française, as you would at home."

Joe wondered what this meant. He hoped it would become clear.

The soup was meaty and strong, but not unpleasant, although it was rather cold. When everyone had finished, they began helping themselves to the rest of the food. That must be what Ellen meant, he thought, self service.

He filled his plate, sticking mainly to the beef, turkey, and apple pie, and taking just a small amount of the other dishes. He still didn't like mixing sweet things with savoury, so he kept them carefully separate on his plate, as he'd done before.

He had never eaten calf's foot jelly, however. So when he braced himself to try it, expecting something beef-flavoured, his taste buds shrank in shock. It was very sweet, with a lemony tang.

Fortunately, Ellen didn't notice him splutter. "I find it interesting," she mused, "that the sugar in that jelly may have come from the plantation where your uncle is at this very moment. It comes from his sugar house, after all." She smiled. "Sugar has made Bristol great, you know, and your uncle is a part of that."

Joe had the feeling that she was trying to impress him. He nodded and picked up his glass. Without thinking, he took a sip, and gagged before he could stop himself. At most other meals in the past, they'd drunk small beer. He didn't like it much, but at least he was used to it. Whatever this was, it was ten times worse: vinegary and sharp, with a nasty metallic taste.

"Do you not drink wine at home, cousin?" teased Peter. "I would have thought the son of a French Count would have a nice glass of white with breakfast, dinner and supper!"

"It's a little different to this," Joe said politely. He remembered the well at Old Wardour castle. "In fact," he said, "we often drink water with meals."

Peter looked surprised, but didn't answer.

Joe said almost nothing else while they ate. Opposite him, Miss Waters was silent too. The familiarity of her face nagged at Joe. He knew he must have met her before, even though her name meant nothing to him. Whoever she'd been, he'd never seen her eat, he realised. He tried to picture her doing something else. Sewing, he thought, and carrying things. There was another memory as well. He stretched around in his mind. He'd been sitting down while she leaned over him, doing something he couldn't see. And the smell. There had been a truly disgusting smell!

Then it came to him! This was Arethusa, Lucy's slave from Roman times. She'd dyed his hair for him. That was the smell, he remembered it now – leeches rotted in red wine! He groaned.

Lucy's mother glanced at him and frowned. But Joe scarcely noticed. Arethusa had taken a huge risk for him, and he'd never thanked her properly. He longed to say something now. But of course, Miss Waters would have no idea what he was talking about.

She saw his smile and dropped her gaze. Joe flushed. He'd embarrassed her. He fixed his attention on his plate and didn't look up until the meal was finished, and Ellen had said Grace again.

Peter returned to school soon afterwards, and Joe assumed that he and Lucy would continue their lessons with Miss Waters. Evidently, Lucy expected this too, because she looked taken aback when Ellen suggested they go for a walk. "The fog has lifted," her mother said. "You should make the most of the afternoon."

Lucy didn't need to be told twice. She hustled Joe downstairs and summoned a maid to bring her hat and boots, and some other thing Joe didn't understand.

"You must have had a redingote too?" she said.

"A redding goat?"

"A top coat of some sort."

"Oh, yes." He wondered if he needed to request his things separately, but the maid reappeared bringing his hat and coat with Lucy's.

Lucy changed her silk slippers and let the maid help her into her coat. It was tightly fitted where it buttoned down to the waist, with a full skirt open to the floor. The hat she was fastening at an angle looked as though the top had been sat on, while the wide brim was curled upwards on both sides and decorated with a mass of ribbons and ostrich feathers. Presumably, this was the height of fashion.

When Lucy was finally ready, Morley held the door open for them both.

"If I'm going to be staying for a while," Joe said, following her down the steps and up the street, "you should probably tell me the names of the roads and places as we go."

"Alright," she agreed, "though there's not much to this walk. This is Park Street. We're number 5."

"Oh, good!"

"Why, 'good'?"

"I mean, it's good that your house has a number," Joe said. "It makes things easier."

She looked puzzled.

"Houses haven't always had numbers, you know," he said.

"I see," she said, clearly not seeing.

At the end of the terrace, they turned left. "This is Great George Street," she told him. "At least it will be when they've finished it."

There were five houses spaced out along the left

hand side of what was really a track rather than a road. Only the first three seemed to be complete, and the last house was still a shell. On the opposite side was a graveyard, and then trees. Joe could see he'd been right earlier in thinking that they were on the edge of Bristol. He could almost feel the wooded hillsides holding out against the city. They would lose soon enough, he thought, a little sadly.

"These first three houses belong to some very wealthy men," Lucy said. "Each house is different inside. That one's got a plunge pool in the basement!"

Joe looked. The house she was pointing at did look quite grand, but not much more so than her own house.

"And you can see these two are going to be even bigger!" She sounded awed.

"How long does it take to build a house?" Joe asked, as they drew level with the unfinished buildings.

"A year or two, I think," Lucy said.

Joe considered this. That wasn't so bad, given that there were no lorries to deliver the materials, no diggers or cement mixers, no power tools. There were just horses and carts, and lots and lots of men with spades and pick axes, digging foundations and passing the earth out in buckets; men hauling vast timbers and blocks of stone up and down the scaffolding with pulleys; men sawing, hammering, chiselling.

Beyond the fifth house, the track petered out.

"We're coming on to Brandon Hill," Lucy said, leading the way along a path that curled round through the trees. "I like coming up here. You get a great view from the top."

For a few minutes, they walked without speaking. Now that the fog had lifted, a pale sun was just visible in the sky. There was nobody else up here, Joe noticed. In his own time, there would have been people out with their dogs, or runners, even on a weekday afternoon. But now he thought about it, that wasn't something he'd ever seen in Lucy's worlds. Perhaps people were too busy. And of course, they didn't need to go out for exercise – they would get plenty just living their normal lives without cars or washing machines or any of the other labour-saving devices he took for granted.

"Here we are!" Lucy announced. The trees had thinned, and they climbed up together to stand on some exposed rocks. "Not bad, is it?"

Joe gazed out. It was like the most vivid painting of the past he could ever have imagined. Below them, the river wound its way in from the coast through forests and fields, forking so that it surrounded the city on three sides. Inside the bend in the river, spires and rooftops crowded together, the smoke from their chimneys rising in dozens of thin, wispy lines.

It looked so quaint, so idyllic. Joe smiled. He knew perfectly well that the past wasn't at all quaint in reality. But he did wish he could take a photograph to take home with him. It was frustrating to know that however hard he tried to remember, this would all become blurred in his head.

"It's amazing!" he said softly.

Lucy looked at him. "You know, I can't get over how much you've changed." She shook her head. "You would never have said that before!"

"I haven't changed, not really," Joe said. He hesitated. This was as good a time as any to tell her that he wasn't Josiah. But he couldn't bear to spoil the moment.

"What are those towers?" he asked instead, pointing to several huge brown cones poking up around the city.

"They're glasshouses," Lucy said.

"But that's not glass, is it? It looks like brick."

She laughed. "It is brick! The glasshouses *make* glass. They're not made of it! The towers are the furnaces."

Joe felt foolish. At home, he was sure a glasshouse was a kind of greenhouse. Of course, greenhouses weren't green. Perhaps his own world wasn't any more logical than this one.

"Bristol is famous for its blue glass," Lucy was saying. "Like the finger bowls and the wine glass rinsers that were on the dinner table – though the glasshouses make normal glass, too. And you see that big building over there?" She pointed. "That's my

66

father's sugar house."

Joe peered through the haze. He wasn't quite sure which building he was looking at, since there were quite a few large ones amongst all the crooked houses.

"There are about a dozen sugar houses," she said. "They're all over the city. Everybody everywhere wants sugar."

Joe nodded. "Your mother said something about a plantation in the West Indies. Does it come here directly from there?"

"Yes." Lucy waved her hand. "Nobody would want it as it is when it arrives though. It's dark and rough. The sugar houses refine it into the beautiful white sugar we had with our tea."

"Where I'm from," Joe said, "sugar comes as a fine powder, like sand."

"We call that Lisbon sugar," Lucy said scornfully. "The yellowish colour shows you it's not as refined."

Joe was about to say that granulated sugar was white, but thought better of it. He gestured to a ring of buildings around a green, as a way of changing the subject. "What's that over there?"

"Queen Square," she replied. "That's where the richest merchants live. And to the left is the old part of Bristol. In medieval times there was a wall around it, but it's mostly gone now."

They stood for a while longer, looking at the

view. Then Lucy pulled out a pendant from inside the neck of her coat. Joe saw with surprise that it was a watch. She'd never had a watch before.

"We should make our way down," she said.

Walking back along the path beside his friend, Joe felt calmer than he had done all day. He'd survived the first few hours here without saying anything too idiotic, and from now on, it would get easier, except for the conversation about who he really was. Even that felt less scary than usual, though.

Then he remembered what he needed to ask Lucy. "Wasn't there an older boy living here when I visited you before?" He frowned, as though it was hard to recall. "He might have been called Tobias or Toby, I'm not sure."

Lucy was thoughtful. "There's no-one in the family called Tobias," she said. "And nobody amongst the servants with that name, as far as I know. Morley and the footmen have been with us for years, and so has the coachman, but it isn't any of them. Could it have been the kitchen boy? They do come and go, but they're usually our age or younger. Are you sure this Tobias was older?"

"Yes, definitely. Never mind," Joe said. "I must have mixed him up with someone else." He kept his voice casual, but he was jubilant. At last, a chance to be with Lucy without Tobias there to spoil things! If he could just keep himself safe, there was no knowing how long he might be able to stay.

But as they reached the end of Great George Street, a hackney carriage was drawing up outside Lucy's house.

"I wonder who that is," she said. "I'm sure my father would have written if he was coming home. And we're not expecting anyone else." She hurried down the road.

Joe followed more slowly. The coachman had jumped down and was opening the door of the carriage. A head appeared. In a heartbeat, Joe knew who it was.

All the same, the shock was like a lightning bolt! Joe could have been looking in a mirror, except that the boy ahead of him was climbing down from the step rather than standing in the street gaping like Joe.

Midway between them, Lucy froze. She stared at the new arrival. Then she swung round to stare at Joe.

His mouth was open but no sound came out. It was exactly like seeing himself outside his own body. The other boy was the same height, the same build. He was wearing the same clothes. But it was the face that was most astonishing of all. He looked identical to Joe. No wonder nobody had realised!

The boy glanced round. He, too, froze.

For what seemed an eternity, the three of them stood motionless on the pavement. Lucy's eyes were wide. The boy's eyes were narrow.

Joe felt himself sway. He heard the hissing begin

in his ears, and swell almost at once to a roar.

Frantically, he fumbled with his cravat. He had to give Lucy his St. Christopher! It might be difficult to come back now the real Josiah de Courson was here. But he didn't want it to be impossible.

There wasn't time to unfasten the catch. Joe yanked the chain. It snapped. He threw it towards Lucy. There was a tinkling sound as the St. Christopher struck the ground.

And then nothing. It rolled towards Lucy, its brightness already dull. Joe saw her pick it up. But she was no more than a shadow. Josiah had faded out. The carriage, the coachman, the street, it had all gone.

Joe felt himself lurch. He tried to concentrate on staying upright. His mind went dark.

Then the roaring subsided. His own world surged back in. He was standing beside the great bronze nail in the centre of Bristol, gripping it so hard his fingers were white as stone.

6

"– it's got two minute hands. The red one shows Greenwich Mean Time and the black one … Joe? Are you alright?" Dad caught hold of Joe's arm. "You've gone an awful colour. You're not going to pass out, are you?"

Joe leaned against his father, glad of his warmth and strength. He waited for the dizziness to stop.

"Are you okay?"

"Fine," Joe croaked. "I just came over a bit faint."

"Let's get you some breakfast quick," Dad said. "It's my fault for dawdling. Come on. We'll go back to that café you suggested."

Joe let his father steer him back the way they'd come. The nausea wasn't too bad, but he was still dazed and disorientated by the suddenness of the time switch.

By the time he'd finished his blueberry muffin however, he was feeling better. "When was the French

Revolution, Dad?" he asked.

His father put his coffee cup down. "One of the things I really like about you," he said, "is that I never know what you're going to ask next! What made you think of that?"

Joe sipped his hot chocolate. "I came across it in a book," he lied. "I wondered what year it was."

"It was actually about ten years," Dad said. "People often think of it as 1789, because that was the start of it, with the storming of the Bastille in Paris. The other bit that people remember came later, when they started beheading people with the guillotine. King Louis XVI was the first, in January 1793, and Queen Marie Antoinette was executed a few months later."

"The guillotine," Joe said. "Is that the frame with the blade?"

Dad nodded. "Huge numbers of people were sent to the guillotine in the later part of the Revolution. A lot of them hadn't done much wrong except for being rich. It was a bit unfair really," he said, seeing Joe's frown.

But Joe was trying to work out what year it had been in Lucy's world. Peter had mentioned the king fleeing, but not his execution, so it had to be before 1793. And it probably wasn't right at the start of the Revolution, because Josiah's parents wouldn't have been worried enough to send him away. After all, they didn't know what was going to happen. Looking back across history, you could fall into the trap of thinking that things were inevitable, as though the events were all mapped out in advance. But that wasn't true. Nobody who lived through something knew how it was going to turn out.

In any case, whether it was 1791 or a year either side probably didn't make a whole lot of difference. It wasn't like last time in London, where it had mattered precisely what date it was.

"What was happening here in the 1790s?" he asked.

"That would have been Georgian England," Dad said. "George III. Or did you mean here in Bristol?"

"Here in Bristol, I suppose," Joe said, "if you know."

"I don't know year for year," Dad said. "But Bristol was a major port throughout the eighteenth century, and at that time, it was up to its neck in the slave trade."

Joe's hot chocolate stopped halfway to his mouth. "Did they trade slaves here, then?"

Dad shook his head. "No slave ship ever landed its human cargo in England, though plenty of people think they did. There are quite a few urban myths in Bristol to do with it: Black Boy Hill, and The Black Boy Inn on Whiteladies Road, for example. They're commonly thought to be related to the slave trade. But 'black boy' was a popular name for lots of places after the black-haired Charles II came back to the throne. So the pub and the road might have been named for him.

And the white ladies of Whiteladies Road might have been medieval nuns in white habits, but they certainly weren't white-skinned ladies with African slaves.

"There's a rather persistent myth about the Redcliffe caves, too, that slaves were chained up there. There's not a shred of truth in that one. The slaving ships sailed from Bristol to Africa with goods to trade, exchanged them for slaves, and sailed directly to the West Indies. That part of the journey, where the slaves were transported, was called the Middle Passage. When the ships came back to Bristol, they were carrying the sugar and tobacco produced by the slaves, but not the slaves themselves. The whole thing is called the Triangular Trade because the route makes a triangle on the map."

Dad paid the bill and they got up to leave.

"If slaves were never traded here, why do you say the city was up to its neck in it?" Joe felt decidedly uneasy.

"Well, there are the obvious things: street names like Jamaica Street and Guinea Street, for example. Guinea was what English merchants called the bit of the African coast where the slavers kidnapped people, including children."

They went down an alleyway beside the café and came out onto a much bigger road. "Then there are the streets named after successful slave traders," Dad went on, "such as Farrs Lane, Cave Street, Elton Street and Elton Road, and the various roads named after

Tyndall. And of course, there's Bristol's most infamous merchant, Edward Colston. He has all sorts named after him."

"Who was he?"

"He was a member of the Society of Merchant Venturers, who fought for slaving ships to be allowed to sail in and out of Bristol. He made a lot of money out of slaving, and most notably gave his name to the Colston Hall, though not during his lifetime. People have been arguing for years about whether the hall should change its name, and it is now going to."

"Why?" Joe asked. "What's the point?"

Dad dug his hands into his pockets as they walked. "Partly, there are people who are really unhappy with the association. There have been bands and artists who refused to play there, and some people won't go to events, because of the name."

"It's just a name, though!"

"For some. But for others, giving Colston's name to a concert hall celebrates him, when he doesn't deserve to be celebrated."

"But if you change the name," Joe said, "isn't that like trying to cover over the past? Like pretending it didn't happen? Wouldn't it be better to leave it, and just make sure that everyone knows what he did, so they don't think he's some kind of hero?"

Dad nodded. "That's the other argument. The trouble is, it's hard to get the message across. People tend to assume automatically that a building has been named after someone who was generous or good. They're not going to stop for a lecture about where that person's money came from.

"The interesting thing about the Colston Hall debate is that it's done more than any education programme could ever have done to make sure people know about Colston."

They turned off down a street to the left.

"It probably is the right thing to do, to change the name," Dad went on. "But if we're going to avoid airbrushing our nation's past then Britain needs to be taught about the way our forefathers behaved."

"Do you mean ordinary people in Bristol back then?" Joe asked. "They couldn't have been involved, could they, if the slaves weren't traded here?" He knew that Lucy's family was much too wealthy to count as 'ordinary'. But he was hoping for reassurance.

"Very few people would have seen it first hand," Dad said. "But that doesn't mean they weren't involved indirectly. Just think about it. First, there's the shipping, so that's all the people who worked around the docks – boat builders and chandlers, rope makers, sail makers, shipping agents, water bailiffs, the men who worked on the wharves. That's a lot of people. Not all ships were slave ships of course. But at its peak, a huge number of the port's comings and goings were connected with slavery in some way.

"Then there were all the people who made the goods that were shipped to Africa to exchange for slaves – brass, copper, glass beads, cloth, even guns.

"And of course, somebody must have been manufacturing the chains, and the manacles and leg irons that were used on the Middle Passage."

"What are manacles?" Joe asked, not sure he wanted to know.

"They're iron bands that were put round a person's wrists and chained together, like very heavy handcuffs," Dad said. "And leg irons were the same thing, only for the ankles. Those poor people were kept chained up for most of the voyage, two or three months, in near darkness on rough seas, in their own and everyone else's filth and sick. It must have been hell on earth! And think of the disease! It's no wonder so many of them died on the crossing. Those who made it to the West Indies alive must have been in a terrible state! But back in this country, there were plenty of people happy to make money out of it."

Joe looked at him, aghast.

"Meanwhile, out in the West Indies," Dad continued, "the plantation owners needed supplies sent over. That's what I meant about other shipping connected with slavery. Clothes, food, building materials and furniture – it was all sent over, as well as all the tools for growing and harvesting the crops, and the barrels for storing it.

"And at the other end of the route, there was what the plantations produced, to be shipped back to England: molasses, rum, tobacco, and most importantly, sugar. You could say that sugar is what made Bristol great."

A shiver ran down Joe's spine to hear Lucy's mother's words repeated in such a different way. "But – " He wanted to stop Dad now. But Dad was just getting into his stride.

"There were lots of buildings called sugar houses around Bristol," he was saying, "where the sugar was refined. That was a complicated process. It would have needed a lot of people to do the work, so all of them were indirectly involved in slavery. Then there were the merchants buying and selling the refined sugar. And because a lot of merchants, and ship owners and plantation owners, got rich from all this, there was a building boom."

He gestured over his shoulder. "We've just come past King Street where the Theatre Royal is. That was built during the eighteenth century. And we're about to come to Queen Square, where some of the richest families in Bristol set up home."

Dad was unknowingly echoing Lucy, too. Joe stood beside him and looked at the gracious houses he'd seen with his friend from Brandon Hill.

"Not all the buildings are the original ones," Dad said. "But the ones that have been replaced are the same style, so it probably feels pretty similar to how it was back then. Except that it's peaceful here now, isn't it? Imagine the industry when it was being built, all those labourers from all the different trades!"

Joe thought of the new houses he had just seen with Lucy.

"Think of all the timbers and bricks being delivered and hoisted up," Dad said. "And inside, the staircases and the chandeliers. You can see how every one of the workmen had a connection to slavery – even the lowliest errand boy on the building site. Because the houses on this square, and a lot of other buildings around Bristol, were built with dirty money."

Joe was silent. Was Lucy's house one of those? He had admired its elegance. He'd enjoyed her family's wealth. Yet in all probability, it had been paid for with people's lives.

"Mind you," Dad said, as they walked along the side of the square, "it wasn't just Bristol. The same money was pouring into London, and Liverpool and Glasgow. All over the country, in fact, there are grand Georgian buildings still standing on their slaving foundations. Some of our institutions, even – our banks and insurance companies, the railways, some of our universities, even the Church of England! All of us benefit pretty much every day, in some form or another. The people of this country owe a huge debt to the millions forced into slavery by our ancestors."

They had reached the corner of the square, and looked back for several long moments without speaking. Joe didn't know what to say. He didn't want to talk about this any more, didn't want to think about it, especially what it might have to do with Lucy. It wasn't her fault, what had happened, any more than it was his. But that didn't make it okay.

They left the square, crossed a wide road and went down a side street which came out beside the river. Plane trees had been planted along what must originally have been the quay. It was empty here now, just a short, misty stretch of water to saunter along. Joe tried to picture it as it had been in Lucy's time, the masts towering in the fog, the quayside crowded and busy. But it was impossible.

"There is one memorial to a slave, rather than a slave owner," Dad said. "Over there."

He pointed at a curved footbridge with two giant horns sticking up from it. "It's called Pero's Bridge," he explained, "after a slave called Pero. That wasn't his real name, of course. But it was the European name he was given when he was sold."

"Why did they do that?" Joe asked, despite himself.

"It was another way of breaking a slave's spirit," Dad said, "as though the rest of it wasn't enough! If you kidnap a person and separate them from their children or parents, and from anyone else who speaks the same language, and you keep them in worse conditions than we would keep an animal, there's a good chance they'll lose the will to fight you. But just in case, you take away their name as well, to make them forget who they used to be."

"What was Pero's real name?"

80

"We don't know. He was brought to England by a trader called John Pinney when he moved home from the West Indies. What's really sad is that Pinney never gave Pero his freedom, so he died a slave. He was only about forty."

Joe sighed. Was there nothing good to be said about anything? "What are those horn things on the bridge?" he asked. "Are they supposed to have a meaning?"

Dad grinned. "No, they're just arty counterweights to balance the bridge when it lifts up to let the big boats through. Shall we go across and up Park Street towards John Pinney's house? It's a museum now. Or shall we leave that till later and go to the M Shed?"

Joe knew he did want to go to Park Street. He might find Lucy's house! But for now, he wanted a break from thinking about her world and its connections with slavery and sugar.

"What's the M Shed?" he asked.

"It's a kind of museum of the city," Dad said. "It seems to have all sorts of things relating to Bristol. It looks really interesting."

"Let's go there, then," Joe agreed. It seemed a good way of putting off the things he didn't want to think about.

But the M Shed had an exhibition on slavery too. Joe hung back as Dad looked round.

"You asked about manacles," he said. "There's a

pair here, and some leg irons as well."

Dad moved on, poring over the artefacts inside the glass cabinets. "Come and look at these account books from the plantations," he said. "This is fascinating!" He leaned closer. "It lists the collars they used to punish slaves, alongside ladles and shutters – just another ordinary item." He glanced across at Joe. "Those collars were made of iron, with long prongs sticking out so that the slave couldn't lie down comfortably. Sometimes they even had cow bells attached. Imagine the weight! And the noise every time you moved, so close to your head!"

Joe tried not to imagine it.

"You'd have thought this plantation owner would have been ashamed to treat another human being so cruelly," Dad said. "If I did something like that, I'd want to hide it. But you can tell from the fact that the collars are on the list that it didn't strike anyone as unusual!" He shook his head.

"And look," he said, turning around. "This big white cone is sugar. It's called a sugarloaf. They used those things like pliers next to it to break bits off. They must have ended up with really jagged fragments of sugar for their tea, don't you think?"

This was too much for Joe. He backed away. "I don't feel very well," he mumbled. "Can we go outside and get some fresh air?"

Dad sprang forward. "Of course! Do you feel sick? There's a bench over there. Sit down. Put your head between your knees."

"I want to go outside," Joe insisted. He did feel sick. But sitting with his head between his knees wouldn't get rid of the memory of Lucy's mother spooning shards of sugar into his teacup. And it wasn't just any old sugar, either! It was sugar from Lucy's father's sugar house. Worse, it had probably been grown on her uncle's slave plantation. His friend was part of something really evil!

Joe closed his eyes, trying to shut out the knowledge. Perhaps he could let this latest world go, and hope to meet Lucy in another time further on in history … except that he'd given her his St. Christopher. He couldn't get to anywhere else in the past without it.

What was more, sooner or later, she'd be bound to call him back. The only way to prevent that happening was to stop thinking about her. And that would mean never seeing her again. His breath caught in his throat. He knew he couldn't forget her just like that, not now.

Outside the M Shed, he hung over the railing beside the river. His stomach swirled like the currents below him. There was nothing for it. He would have to let things take their course.

And when she summoned him back, he would try and make her see what was wrong with her world.

7

Joe and Dad spent Saturday afternoon at @Bristol, so it wasn't until the next morning that they set out to see more of the city. It was clear and bright, not as early as the previous day, because Dad had insisted on cooking a huge breakfast for them at the apartment.

"We can't have you flaking out again!" he said.

Joe smiled faintly. Bacon wasn't going to save him, and anyway, he wasn't sure this morning that he wanted to be saved. He still felt very nervous at the prospect of confronting Lucy about her family's involvement in slavery. But that wasn't going to go away. It would be better really to just get on with it.

They walked down King Street, past some almshouses, the Theatre Royal and several Tudor buildings, all of which must have existed in Lucy's time, Joe guessed. But when they came out onto Broad Quay, there wasn't a quay any more. There wasn't even a river! Now, it was an open plaza with fountains and benches, and trees dotted around. Try as he might, Joe couldn't match it to anything he'd seen in Lucy's world.

"We'll go across here," Dad said. "We could look into the cathedral, though there's probably a service on since it's Sunday. Or there's the Georgian House Museum I mentioned yesterday – the sugar merchant's house. Shall we have a look?"

"Maybe." Joe paused. "I did wonder if we might walk up onto the hill, if you still can."

"What do you mean, if you still can? Which hill?"

Joe pointed in what felt like the right direction. "There was a road off Park Street that led up onto it, I thought." He tried to keep his voice vague but his information still sounded oddly precise, considering he wasn't supposed to know Bristol. "I saw something on a map," he added, unconvincingly.

"That sounds like Brandon Hill. Fancy you noticing that! It's not all that big. But yes, we could certainly walk up to the Cabot Tower. I can think of worse things to do on a lovely morning."

Joe's eyes were out on stalks as they walked on now. He was fairly sure they had joined the route he'd taken yesterday in the carriage with Hannah and Mary. Most of it was completely unrecognisable, and yet there were occasional corners - a pub here, a row of buildings there - that he thought he'd seen in Lucy's world. It was strange to find them in such a different setting. They looked small and fragile among the newer buildings. And yet, they weren't fragile really. These were the survivors, anchor points against the rising tide of change.

"This is College Green," Dad said, as they reached the triangle of grass Joe had passed in the carriage. "I think I pointed it out on Friday night."

Joe gazed across the green, just as puzzled as when he'd been with Lucy. In her time, there had been a small church at the tip of the triangle, which was now gone. And he'd been right about the cathedral – it was definitely whole now, where in the past, at least half of it had been missing. Not yet built, he supposed.

"It's such a trip down memory lane for me," Dad said. "That big tower up there at the top of the road is one of the main university buildings, so all this was my stamping ground."

"And we're going up Park Street?"

Dad nodded. Joe looked at the road ahead. "I thought it was steeper," he said, remembering the dip in the road and the horses and carriages ploughing up the other side.

"Believe me," Dad laughed, "when you're late for a lecture this is steep enough!"

But Joe wasn't listening. There was a bridge here now, he saw, right where the dip had been. He wouldn't have noticed it at all if he hadn't been looking. But this must explain the change, because the cross street underneath was a long way down, while

Park Street had been smoothed out over the top.

He started hunting for numbers. All of the buildings on both sides were now cafés or shops. They seemed to have offices and flats above them, some expensive-looking, others grimy, with torn curtains at their windows.

But the first number he could see was 11. Then came a side road, and then a large building with columns and a frieze of Greeks or Romans above the entrance. Joe was positive he hadn't seen it with Lucy, even though it looked as though it could have been there.

"What's that?" he asked.

"I think it's the Freemasons Hall," Dad said. "They're a rather secretive organisation, which is why it's not marked."

Beyond, came number 33. There was no number 5, nor anything close.

Joe struggled to hide his disappointment. Lucy's house had gone. He turned on the pavement to look back down the road, just to be certain. And without warning, the rushing sound filled his ears.

He crouched down quickly, as though he was tying his shoelaces. With luck, that would give him a few moments to recover when he got back later.

Then all thought of later was gone, swept away with his own world. The cars and buses, the shops and cafés with their music, the hum of the electric city, all replaced by the rumble of cartwheels and men shouting.

For the second time in two days, Joe felt dazed by the abruptness of the change. He moved to hold onto some railings and waited until he felt steadier.

He was standing outside the house next door to Lucy's. This must be the spot he'd disappeared from last time. He looked both ways. It also seemed to be just a few metres further up from where he'd crouched down in his own world. So he must have been right outside her house, all dejected at not finding number 5! He grinned. The street had just been renumbered at some point. Why hadn't he thought of that?

Horses were heaving carts and carriages up the road, which was indeed steeper than it would be in the future. Joe looked round in the direction he'd been going with Dad. The top half of Park Street wasn't there. Nor was the tower that Dad had pointed out. In their place were the trees he'd noticed when he arrived last time, and between them, open ground.

He glanced down at himself. His shoes and stockings were still spattered with mud from the walk with Lucy on Brandon Hill. But the air was much milder now than it had been that day. It felt like late afternoon, with no sign of it getting dark. The road was running with water, and there a freshness behind the usual smells of manure and wood smoke.

At that moment, the door of Lucy's house opened and she appeared at the top of the steps with her brother. Peter was looking the other way and didn't see Joe, but Lucy noticed him at once. She said something to Peter, who went back inside the house.

"Josiah?" she called, looking intently at Joe.

For a split-second, Joe was confused. Then the memory of those last bizarre moments came flooding back. Where was the real Josiah now? Not in Lucy's house, presumably, or she wouldn't expect to see him in the street. So did that mean that Joe should pretend to be Josiah again? Could they both be here at the same time? Joe couldn't imagine how. Just seeing Josiah had been enough to eject him from Lucy's world.

He stood, rooted to the spot. As ever, he felt totally unprepared.

Lucy trotted down the steps. "You're not him, are you?" she said softly. "You're the other one." She held out her hand. In her palm was Joe's St. Christopher. "I was just wondering about you. I've had this inside my redingote since that day. Every time I've found it, I've thought of you."

Joe nodded, but didn't take the pendant from her.

"Don't you want it back?"

"Not yet," he said. "I can explain."

She shook her head. "Later," she said, tucking the St. Christopher away. "We only have a minute before Peter comes back out. You need to do as I say."

Joe nodded again, wondering what he was agreeing to.

"This time, you have to put on a French accent when you speak," she said. "Don't smile. And try to be surly, rude even."

"But I'm not normally like that," Joe protested. "Nobody will like me."

"Nobody likes Josiah either!" Lucy retorted. "If you're going to pass yourself off as him, you have to behave like he does."

"What if I don't want to?"

"What choice do you have?" she asked sharply. "If you pretend to be him, everything will be much easier. We'll talk about who you actually are later. In the meantime, I'll help you," she added more gently. "You were nice. I'd have much preferred it if you'd stayed instead of him. It was no wonder I thought you'd changed. The real Josiah turned out to be just as nasty as he'd been before!"

"But he's not here now?" Joe asked. "I thought he was staying for a long time."

Lucy snorted. "It feels like he was here years, but it was only two and a half months. Fortunately, he announced yesterday that he was leaving. We're all delighted to see the back of him. Well, nearly all of us."

"So if I'm supposed to be him, what do we tell them about why I've come back?"

"Change of heart," Lucy said quickly. "Here comes Peter. Leave it to me."

Joe looked up to see Lucy's brother coming

down the steps at the front of the house. "Cousin Josiah!" Peter exclaimed. "Back so soon!" His voice was cold.

Joe tried to set his expression to be disagreeable. It felt all wrong. He'd always got on well with Peter before.

"The ship ran aground at Shirehampton," Lucy said. "He's walked back."

"Why not wait on board for the tide to turn?" Peter asked sourly. "You made it quite plain you didn't want to stay any longer."

"I 'ad a change of 'eart," Joe said, in a horribly bogus French accent. "I sought per'aps it was a sign from God, zat I was meant to be 'ere."

Peter grimaced. Joe wondered whether it was the accent, or the prospect of having his cousin back again.

"Lucy and I were going for a walk," Peter said, "now that the rain has stopped." He peered at Joe suspiciously. "You look remarkably dry for someone who's walked so far on a day like today."

Joe decided it was safest to shrug and say nothing.

"I dare say you won't want to join us," Peter prompted him. "You must be tired."

Joe thought quickly. He had no desire to go into Lucy's house without her, or to have to explain himself without knowing what had happened in his absence. "Actually, now that it's a nice afternoon," he said, "a walk would be pleasant." He realised halfway through speaking that he'd forgotten the accent already, and tried to put it on for the last few words without knowing quite how it should sound.

Peter raised an eyebrow. "A reformed character," he said, with deep sarcasm. "I'd never have thought that being washed up could improve someone's manners so much!" He spun on his heel and set off up the street.

Lucy gave Joe a pointed look. What was that supposed to mean, he wondered anxiously. Was he doing such a bad job of impersonating Josiah? Or was she trying to tell him to pick up on Peter's remarks about improved manners, and be a little nicer? It was going to be uncomfortable otherwise, having to behave so differently to usual. Already Joe was wishing he hadn't agreed. After all, Lucy seemed to have accepted that he'd appeared out of the blue, so why wouldn't Peter? Except, of course, that Peter hadn't seen him disappear.

This time, they walked on up Park Street, past the road Joe had taken with Lucy last time.

"We thought we'd walk through the park around the Royal Fort," Lucy said, seeing Joe's glance. "We wanted to have a look at the big new building project."

Joe nodded but didn't speak.

They continued up the road in silence. Waves of irritation and dislike seemed to be pulsing through the air from Peter. Joe wished he could do something about it. Lucy kept shooting looks his way too, but he guessed she didn't want to ask him anything in front of her brother.

The upper part of Park Street was a building site, just as the end of the side road had been before. Joe thought of what Dad had said about the building boom coming from slave money. He pushed the thought to the back of his mind. That would have to wait.

Beyond the end of Park Street, they turned off across a common, mostly cleared of trees but still thick with long grass. The path lead through a gate and onto park land, where several groups of men were digging trenches in an expanse of clipped grass.

Above, at the top of the rise, a mansion looked down over all of Bristol. "That's Royal Fort House," Lucy said. "Thomas Tyndall has just sold it. They're going to build several crescents of houses on the land."

Tyndall, Joe thought grimly. That had been one of the names Dad had mentioned. Thomas Tyndall must have made his money from the slave trade. How quickly the connection had come up, now that he knew about it!

Peter huffed. "I don't know why you're telling our cousin all this! If he cared, he'd know already. We must have discussed it half a dozen times in front of him!"

Lucy looked away. Joe realised she had been explaining for his benefit.

"Is your fazzer back yet?" he asked, to change the subject. He was congratulating himself on remembering to use the accent, when he saw that the question itself had been a mistake. If Lucy's father had returned from his voyage while Josiah had been staying, he couldn't fail to know. And if not, it was hardly likely to have happened in the few hours that Josiah had been gone. Joe felt colour spread across his cheeks.

Peter growled again. But Lucy came to Joe's rescue. "He came home from the sugar house in time for dinner," she said, as though he had been asking something slightly different. "He's working in his study this afternoon. You know how busy it is since he came home three weeks ago."

Joe knew she'd added the last three words to give him the hint he needed. He waited for Peter to object again. But Lucy's brother had brightened. He was waving to someone on the far side of the park.

"That's Henry Cunningham and his brother," he said. "I must go and say hello. You'll be alright with Cousin Josiah, won't you Lucy?" He pulled a face.

"Of course!" she answered. "Do go. We'll see you back at home."

Surprise flashed across Peter's face at his sister's willingness to be left. But he hurried away across the grass without a backwards look.

"Phew!" Lucy grinned. "That was a stroke of luck! There's so much I want to ask you, but I didn't think I'd get the chance." She watched her brother's retreating figure. "I knew he wouldn't be over the moon to see Josiah back again. But he reacted even worse than I expected. I suppose it comes of knowing he'll have to put up with the two of you again."

"The two of me?"

"Sorry," Lucy laughed. "I meant you two cousins. My father brought my aunt and her son back from Jamaica with him. I'd never met this other cousin before. But he's turned out to be even more unpleasant than you ... I mean, Josiah."

"Oh dear. Is he supposed to be my cousin, too?"

"No. He's from the other side of the family. You didn't meet him until we did, last month. His name is Tobias. I'll tell you about him in a bit. But first, I want to know all about you. Who on earth are you?"

But Joe was staring at her, open-mouthed.

"Tobias!" he exclaimed in dismay. "Oh no! Not Tobias!"

8

"What do you mean, not Tobias? You don't know him, do you?"

Joe couldn't find the words. It felt so unfair to have his hopes dashed so soon. Why had he let himself believe that Tobias wasn't here? He should have known better!

At last, he said tightly, "Do you remember, when I was here before, I asked you if there was someone called Tobias?"

"So you did!" Lucy said. "I'd forgotten. And there wasn't then. But there is now." She was clearly intrigued.

"The thing is," Joe went on, "Tobias is always in your worlds." His heart was in his shoes. This wasn't the best place to start explaining who he was. But he had to begin somewhere.

"My worlds?" Lucy frowned. "What on earth are you talking about?"

"I'm from the future," Joe said. Before she could

interrupt, he went on quickly, "The St. Christopher I gave you as I disappeared, that's the key. It takes me back to different times in the past. And you're always there. So is your family. But so is Tobias."

As he'd expected, Lucy looked at him with utter incomprehension. He sighed. It was always like this. In fact, it was remarkable that she ever accepted him at all. The only comfort was that at least this time, she wouldn't be angry with him for pretending to be someone he wasn't.

He took a deep breath. "I've met you before," he said, "all of you. But you won't remember me. You never do. It doesn't matter really. It's not important." For the first time ever, he wondered why he'd bothered to tell her. Perhaps next time, if there *was* a next time, he should keep it to himself. It probably wouldn't change anything.

For several seconds, Lucy was silent. Then she said, "Prove it!"

Joe thought for a moment. The last three times he'd had to persuade her, he'd used the fact that he knew about the death of her younger brother, years ago. He might as well try the same approach now.

"You had a brother called Francis, who died," he said.

She stuck out her chin. "No, I didn't."

"Perhaps not Francis then. But something similar. Freddy? Frank?"

"No."

97

Joe was taken aback. "Are you sure?"

"I think I'd know!"

Joe hesitated. This was absolutely not what he'd expected. "Well, then," he pressed on, "you also had a sister who died, called Anne."

"So what? Of course you know about her! You used her easel, after all."

Joe faltered. "Alright, what about your older brother and sister, Matthew and Cecily? Both of them died, too. Nobody has mentioned them, have they?"

A strange expression appeared on Lucy's face. Joe watched her apprehensively.

"How did you know about them?" Lucy's voice shook.

"Why wouldn't I?" Joe asked. "I've met them several times. I knew them – not very well, but well enough."

"You couldn't have! My mother has lost several babies, two of them before I was born. Matthew was four months old, and Cecily was just six weeks. They would both have been older than Peter. And there was another baby, too, still-born when I was little. I don't think he even had a name. I only know about any of them because my mother mourns them on their birthdays, just like she mourns Anne and Thomas."

Joe was confounded. "Four months?" he repeated. "Six weeks? But Matthew was a grown man. He was supposed to –" Joe broke off. He'd been going to say that Matthew had been supposed to sail on the

Mary Rose when it sank. But that was another world. In this one, he and Cecily hadn't even reached childhood. Joe felt a pang of sadness at the thought of the people they should have become. He'd liked them both. He knew what had been lost in a way that Lucy couldn't.

"What do you mean, Thomas?" he asked instead. "I thought he was at home with his nurse."

"Not *that* Thomas," Lucy said. "Didn't you realise? He was about three when you were last here, wasn't he?"

Seeing Joe's confusion, she corrected herself. "Not you, of course. Josiah. The first Thomas was three when Josiah was last here. Sorry, you do look so like him, I still can't keep you apart in my head. Anyway," she sighed, "Thomas died a year and a half ago, of smallpox. Peter and I were inoculated, but then my mother heard of a child who died from it, so Anne and Thomas weren't. They died within two weeks of each other."

Joe rubbed his forehead. He hadn't realised that anyone knew about inoculation in the 1700s, but that wasn't the most baffling thing. "You do still have a little brother called Thomas, don't you?" he asked.

"It's not the same child," Lucy said. "Baby Thomas isn't yet quite a year old. My mother felt him move inside her on the day the first Thomas died. So she gave him the same name."

They walked on in silence for a while. Joe tried

to imagine his parents having eight children and losing five of them. People in Lucy's time must be so frightened when their children got ill.

Presently, he asked, "What date is it today?"

Lucy was bewildered by the change of subject. "The twenty-first of April," she said. "Why?"

"And what year?"

"1792. But I don't see what that has to do with anything."

"Not the year, maybe," Joe answered, although he felt private satisfaction that he'd worked it out more or less right. "But I do know that you must have had a birthday since I was last here. It's at the end of March, isn't it?" He felt proud that he'd managed to dig this fact out of his memory. Lucy had only ever mentioned her birthday once, when he met her at Old Wardour.

"That's right." She still sounded guarded. "But of course you'd know. We did celebrate it, after all!"

"Not with me, remember? I was here in February, and you and I definitely didn't talk about birthdays then. We didn't even talk about how old you are, although I know you're twelve like me."

Lucy frowned. "I still don't see how it's possible that you already know me," she persisted.

Joe smiled ruefully. "It isn't possible for someone to disappear into thin air, is it? But you saw me do that, too!"

Her brow furrowed even more. "How did that happen?" she asked.

"I'm not completely sure," Joe said. "Usually, it's when I'm in danger that I get pulled back into my own world. This time, I think it was the shock of seeing my double. Josiah does look just like me, doesn't he?"

Lucy grinned. "It was weird, wasn't it? You can see why we thought you were him when you arrived. But why did you go along with it? Why not say who you were from the start?"

"And have a conversation like this with everyone, right at the beginning?" Joe laughed. "No thanks! It's bad enough now with just you! Anyway, Josiah and I have almost the same name. I'm Joe, short for Joseph. When Hannah called to me in town, I misheard her. By the time she'd swept me up, it felt too late to say anything."

Lucy nodded. "It was funny, in a way," she said, "how bemused everyone was when the real Josiah arrived. There he was, complaining loudly about not being met at the quay when everyone thought he'd been with us all day and had just come in from a walk. And of course, his accent was very noticeable, whereas you didn't have an accent at all."

Joe couldn't help but smile. "That's because I'm not French! So what did they think had happened?"

"My mother put it down to Josiah being overtired. That didn't make sense, of course. But how else could she explain it? She hadn't seen you vanish, so it didn't dawn on her that you and Josiah were two different people."

"And what did Josiah think? He saw me, didn't he? He was looking straight at me."

"I never asked him. I decided to pretend nothing had happened. Maybe he put it down to being tired as well! He never mentioned it."

"So what do we do now?"

"Well, I think it would be better if we didn't tell the rest of the family that you're not Josiah."

"What about Peter?" Joe protested. "I hate it that he dislikes me so much!"

Lucy tutted in mock disapproval. "In that case, you should pretend to be someone nice next time! You know, it was obvious within seconds that the real Josiah was the same as he'd always been. My mother couldn't hide her astonishment at the change that seemed to have come over him."

"What do you mean?"

"Well, you'd been so polite and friendly while we drank tea, and over lunch. You might not have said very much, but you seemed glad to be there. Then we went out for a walk together. And as far as my mother could see, you became rude and demanding from the moment we got back. By the way, are you sure you don't want your St. Christopher?"

She pulled it out again from inside her coat.

"Not now," Joe said. "It's how you call me here, by holding it and thinking about me at the same time as I think about you."

She looked dubious. "Does that work?"

"It did today, didn't it? That was exactly what happened."

They had walked all the way to the other side of the park while they were talking, and had looped round, back to where Peter had left them. Now they started back towards Lucy's house, retracing their earlier steps.

"Anyway," Joe said, "it sounds like quite a bit has happened here since I was last with you. Why don't you tell me about that?"

Lucy nodded. "You got the hint about my father coming back from the West Indies?"

"Sorry about the idiotic question," Joe said sheepishly.

"Never mind. Peter's probably forgotten already. In any case, I think you knew that my father went out to deal with his brother's affairs."

"The plantation?"

"That's right. My uncle had left it to my Aunt Katherine and my cousin, Tobias."

"So why did they come back with your father?"

"Aunt Katherine didn't want to stay on out there," Lucy said. "She never liked Jamaica. Tobias wants to take the plantation over, but he's only seventeen. He'll have to be twenty-one before he's legally allowed to."

"I bet he's delighted to be here, then!"

Lucy glanced across at Joe, then realised he was joking. "He's furious!" She chuckled. "He hates

England! He was sent to school over here when he was ten, but he ran away and got himself on a ship back to Jamaica."

"Wow! That was pretty determined!"

"Yes, wasn't it? Anyway, as you can imagine, our house isn't the easiest place to be at the moment, with him like a permanent thundercloud. And it's even worse than it might have been, because the servants are all out of sorts as well."

"Why?" Joe asked. "Is Tobias rude to them?"

Lucy waved a hand. "Of course he is! So was Josiah. But it's not that. They're used to that sort of thing. No, it's because they've had to make way for four more people in the house as well as my aunt and cousin. My father brought a Negro manservant back with him, plus two Negro children and their nursemaid. All four of them were slaves on the plantation."

Joe caught his breath. "The children were slaves too?"

Lucy nodded. "Their mother was a slave, so they were born slaves. Rose is seven, Billy is four. He was just starting to work when my father arrived."

"A four year old slave!" Joe exclaimed. Dad had said children were taken as slaves, but Joe realised he hadn't quite believed him. "Was your uncle a good master?"

Lucy pressed her lips together. "I don't think so. But of course, if you don't beat a slave, they won't work." It sounded as though she was repeating something she'd been told. "And without slaves to work the plantations, we wouldn't have sugar."

Joe paused to look out over the city, glowing in the late afternoon sunshine. "You wouldn't have half of this either," he said, more to himself than to her.

They reached the top of Park Street and walked down it together without speaking. The water that had been streaming down the road had dwindled to a series of trickles, but there were deep channels between the paving stones where it had passed through.

As they came to Lucy's house, she said, "Remember now, Joe who is not Josiah: French accent, surly and unfriendly, just polite enough that they take you back. They won't be pleased to see you, either the servants or the family." She pulled the bell-pull.

At once, the door was opened. "Miss Lucy." Morley bowed. "And Master Josiah again!" He didn't bow to Joe.

Joe did his best to look sullen. If Josiah had been rude to the servants, he shouldn't explain himself to them either.

"I'll tell the mistress you're here."

"Thank you," Joe said automatically. He felt Lucy nudge him. Perhaps he shouldn't even have said that.

But Lucy hissed, "Accent!"

A few moments later, Lucy's mother came out

into the hall. "Josiah!" she exclaimed. "This is unexpected! Did your ship not sail?"

Joe took off his hat and bowed. "It did, Madame," he replied in a voice that he hoped might pass for French. "But we ran aground in ze night. I was sleeping. But I 'ad a dream zat I was being punished for my ingratitude. You 'ave been most kind to me and I 'ave been ungrateful. When I woke and found ze ship aground, I knew it was a sign zat I should not 'ave left."

Joe's heart was pounding. Ellen's face gave nothing away.

"If you will allow me to stay wiz you once again," he pushed on, "I will try to be more … how do you say … appreciative." He bowed again.

Lucy's mother blinked. "Of course," she said.

Joe held his breath, waiting for her to say more. Surely she would identify him as an imposter! His accent sounded terrible, even to his own ears.

But Ellen went on, "Nobody goes through life without needing a second chance. You're welcome to stay, as before. What of your luggage?"

Joe tensed.

"It will have gone with the ship, won't it?" Lucy suggested.

"No matter," Ellen said briskly. "We will lend you what you need for now. Perhaps your mother will return the trunk. I wrote to her yesterday to inform her of your sudden departure. I shall write again and tell her you've changed your mind."

"No, no! I will do it!" Joe said hastily. "I owe 'er an explanation." It would cause even more trouble if Ellen wrote to say Josiah was still here when he was actually back at home.

"Very well." Ellen turned to Lucy. "Where is your brother?"

"He saw Henry Cunningham in the park. Josiah had already joined us, so Peter went to speak to his friends."

"Avoidance," Lucy's mother said shortly. "Josiah, make yourself at home again." She went back into the parlour and closed the door behind her.

Joe let his breath whistle out. "Thank goodness that's over," he muttered. "What now?"

9

Lucy handed her coat and hat to a maid and sat down to take her boots off.

Morley stood silently nearby. Joe gave his hat and coat to the maid as well, and straightened his wig. "Would there be some other shoes I could borrow?" he whispered to Lucy. "Mine are very muddy."

Lucy looked up. "Morley, could you have Amos bring up a full set of clothes for my cousin and clean his shoes for him? Take your shoes off, Josiah. I'll take you up to your room."

As she led the way towards the stairs, Joe murmured, "I need you to tell me what the different rooms are. Everyone will assume I know this house."

Lucy nodded. She began to climb the stairs slowly, waiting until Morley and the maid had gone. Then she stopped and turned around. "My mother's in the parlour," she said, gesturing to the furthest door on the right. "That was where we had tea, remember? The library, where we did painting, is also my father's study. He's working in there, as he often does in the afternoons." She gestured to the door opposite. "And that's the withdrawing room."

"What's the door beside the front door?" Joe asked.

"That's the powder room, remember? Where the water closet is."

"Oh, yes. So where's the kitchen?"

"The kitchens," Lucy replied, emphasising the 's', "are below stairs with the other rooms the servants use. The laundry is done down there, and other household things." Joe could tell she had no idea what those other things were.

"How do you get to it?"

"You don't. But the servants come up through the door next to the powder room. If you need something, ring the bell in whichever room you're in, and a servant will come."

She went on up to the first floor. Joe followed, holding tight to the handrail. The polished stairs felt slippery beneath his stockinged feet.

"You remember, we eat in the dining room up here." Lucy nodded to the open door ahead of them. "Then, this room is Peter's, which is where you'll sleep. We'll come back here in a minute, but I'll quickly show you the rest of the house first. My parents sleep in the largest bedroom, through that door there, with Thomas in his crib. Thomas' nurse, Sarah, used to have the room next door to them, but Tobias is in there now."

"What, right now?"

She smiled. "No, right now he's probably out. There's no school on Saturday afternoons, and Tobias always goes out, even though my father suggested he might spend the time studying with Miss Waters." She lowered her voice. "Peter says he can barely read or write. It seems like he had hardly any education in the West Indies." She looked suddenly uncomfortable. "I didn't mean … Not like you! You could read even though you couldn't write."

"Me?" Joe was momentarily baffled. "Oh! You mean with the quill?" He grinned. "I can write perfectly well with the pens we have at home, but I've never had to use a quill, let alone cut one!"

"What are your pens made of, then?"

"Plastic."

"What's that?"

He shook his head. "It's not worth trying to explain."

Lucy looked at him thoughtfully. "But you'd learnt to paint. Does everyone learn, where you come from?"

"Not everyone. But they teach art in most schools and it makes no difference whether you're a boy or a girl."

"Josiah couldn't paint to save his life!" Lucy's eyes danced. "Miss Waters invited him to join our lesson after you'd done so well. You should have seen the mess he made before he stormed out! Miss Waters couldn't understand it!"

Joe felt a glow of pride mixed with glee.

Lucy led the way onwards up the second flight of stairs. On the next landing were five normal doors, plus a narrower door to one side. There had been a door like this in the same place on the first floor.

"What's in there?" he asked.

"That's the servants' staircase and the butler's lift."

"Morley gets his own lift?" Joe was amazed.

"No!" Lucy laughed. "A butler's lift is for sending food and things up and down between floors. It's what's behind that extra door in the dining room."

Joe recalled the dishes appearing. They must have come quite some way from the kitchen. No wonder the food hadn't been very hot.

"Miss Waters is in here, if you remember," Lucy was saying, "and the room next door is mine. I used to share it with Anne, but my Aunt Katherine sleeps in with me now. It's not really right for her to have to share, but my mother didn't know where else to put her.

"Then, that one's the nursery, which is also where Sarah sleeps. She had to give up her room to Tobias, which didn't go down well. And Hannah got moved out too, from that one there, to make way for Rose and Billy, and their Negro nursemaid, Florence."

Lucy paused. "The one next door is Mary, the

housekeeper. She's important enough to keep her own bedroom, though it would be much too small for Aunt Katherine anyway. Morley has his own room as well, up in the attics. But the footmen have had to share up there, because my father insisted that the new manservant, Amos, should have his own room. That's what I meant about the servants being out of sorts. Most of them have lost their own bit of space, and six extra people in the house means a lot more work, too."

"Don't Amos and Florence do some of the work though?" Joe asked. "They're servants, aren't they?"

"Yes," Lucy said, "but they're having to learn our ways, and they speak a strange kind of English, especially Florence. We don't always understand what she says, nor she us. And even when Amos and Florence *are* working, our servants resent it. Florence looks after Rose and Billy, and Sarah is afraid my parents will ask her to look after Thomas too, which will mean she isn't needed any more."

"What about Amos?"

"That's not much better." Lucy sighed. "Morley's nose is out of joint because Amos has taken over as my father's personal manservant, and the footmen, Jackson and Metcalfe, loathe him for having forced them to share a room." She gave a wry smile. "They're so full of themselves, with their fancy livery. They think they're a cut above everyone else because they have much less work to do. I don't really know why my father keeps them. All they do is wait at table and ride on the back of the carriage when my parents go out." She giggled. "Do you know what people call footmen?"

"What?"

"Fart catchers!"

Joe burst out laughing. "Why?" he spluttered.

"Because all they do is stand behind their master – at the table or on the carriage – as though they're waiting to catch his farts!"

They both broke into wails of helpless laughter.

Downstairs, a door opened. "Is that you, Lucy?" Ellen called up the stairwell.

Joe clapped his hand over his mouth.

"Yes, Mother." Lucy's voice came out as a squeak. She and Joe doubled up again.

"Are you alright? You're not crying, are you?"

"No, Mother," Lucy called back. "I'm fine." But tears streamed down her cheeks as she tried to control herself.

The door downstairs closed again. Joe pulled himself together. "What will she think?"

"Goodness knows!" Lucy wiped her eyes. "There hasn't been much to laugh about round here in a while."

Back on the first floor, they went into Peter's room. There were two beds in here, one of them a four-poster hung with curtains, the other without posts, and stripped of its covers. Joe sat down heavily on this second bed, still weak from laughing.

"Amos will bring some clothes for you in a moment," Lucy said, throwing herself down in the chair by the window.

All at once, Joe remembered Pero. His merriment ebbed away. "Is Amos a free man now?" he asked. "Or is he still a slave?"

Lucy looked up, surprised. "I don't know," she said. "Slave or servant doesn't make much difference, does it? My father treats him well, so I think he's happy to be here, even though the other servants give him the cold shoulder."

Joe considered this. A bit of unfriendliness would be nothing compared to the harshness of life on a plantation. But still the damp English spring must have come as a shock. Amos and Florence couldn't help but feel alien here. It was hardly home sweet home!

And the question of freedom wasn't something you could dismiss just like that, he thought, even though he could see why Lucy might think it made no difference. After all, if the work was the same and you had a good master, why should it matter? If he was free, Amos might choose to stay. But he would be *choosing*. Joe felt sure that was important. He couldn't imagine being someone else's property, owned like an animal.

There was a slight sound from the doorway. A man entered the room, carrying Joe's shoes in one hand and some clothes over his other arm. Seeing Joe, he stopped and bowed. Joe scrambled to his feet and bowed in return. This must be Amos. But except for being black, he was not at all as Joe had imagined him.

He gazed at the manservant in astonishment. Unconsciously, he had assumed that Amos would seem old and broken from years of mistreatment. But the man in front of him stood tall and straight. His shoulders were broad, and though he was thinner than he ought to be, his bearing suggested tremendous strength. His eyes were dark pools in a wide, handsome face, and he was immaculately dressed in a tailcoat and breeches with a wig of black hair tied in a ponytail.

Joe flushed, mortified to have been caught even thinking about someone 'owning' such an impressive man.

But Lucy was unconcerned that Amos might have overheard them talking about him. "How are you today?" she asked him.

Amos' handsome face broke into a smile that lit up the room. "I am well, thank you, Miss Lucy." He pronounced the words with a heavy accent, but his voice was deep and rich.

Joe took an involuntary step backwards. No wonder the footmen disliked him! They'd been a weaselly pair, bowing and scraping to their mistress. Whereas this man … If a man such as this chose to serve you, it would be a great honour! Yet, here was the question again: *had* he chosen? Watching Amos,

Joe knew that his instinct had been right. It did matter, very much.

Amos put down the shoes and began to lay out the clothes he'd brought. "Would Master Josiah like help to dress?" he asked. Joe noticed that his tone was suddenly careful.

He blushed again. He couldn't ask this man to help him! And yet, there might be difficult fastenings on some of these clothes.

Before he could answer, Lucy spoke for him. "Thank you, Amos." She turned away to look out of the window.

Awkwardly, Joe allowed Amos to help him out of his coat and waistcoat. While Amos untied his cravat, he averted his eyes. But when he sat down on the bed to remove his stockings, and Amos knelt to do it for him, Joe flinched. This was not right! It might only be what was expected, but he wasn't the lord of the manor. And even if he were, it was demeaning for a grown man to do such a thing for anyone, especially a man like this one.

Nonetheless, he was changed and ready much more quickly than he would have been without help. "Thank you, Amos," he said meekly.

"You are welcome, Master Josiah." Amos smiled, and this time, warmth shone out towards Joe. "I will ask the maid to make up your bed again."

"Thank you." Joe dropped his gaze to the floor. He felt small and humble.

"Shall we go up to the nursery and see Thomas?" Lucy suggested. Joe raised his head again. Amos had gone without a sound.

The nursery was a bright, pleasant room overlooking the garden. As usual, a fire burned in the grate, though it wasn't all that warm in the room. Cold seemed to be coming from one corner in particular, where a woman sat sewing. At her feet, a baby played with some wooden bricks. This must be Sarah. Joe saw her put on a smile as Lucy looked her way, but her eyes were hostile.

Lucy crouched down beside the baby. "Hello, Tommy," she said, piling the bricks into a tower.

Joe stood uneasily behind her. What would Josiah do? He wouldn't get down on the floor to play, Joe was sure.

On the far side of the room, a young black woman sat on the rug with two more children. This must be Florence with Rose and Billy. The children were doing a complicated kind of knitting on their fingers. Joe looked at them curiously. They weren't what he thought of as black. At least, they were nowhere near as dark-skinned as Florence or Amos. These children had skin the colour of milky coffee.

Florence was singing softly to them, a simple tune with words Joe couldn't understand.

"She's like that all day," Sarah said acidly. "Twittering away like some blooming bird! Should be teaching them English songs if they're going to stay.

English!" she said loudly to Florence. "English!"

Florence bowed her head and stopped singing.

"She'll start up again in a minute, you'll see. You can't shut her up. She's as happy as a pig in muck! An easy life for her, it is now! Ought to be sent back to the plantation where she came from. I heard they beat them there, if they don't do as they're told," Sarah said with relish. "A good flogging might teach her to keep quiet!"

Joe looked across Florence. Her face was turned away from Sarah, but from where he stood, he saw an expression of intense pain. Sarah might not think Florence understood, but it was clear that she did. Then again, maybe Sarah knew full well.

He waited for Lucy to say something, to tell the nursemaid not to be so nasty, perhaps. But Lucy stayed silent, concentrating fiercely on Tommy's bricks.

Deliberately, he crossed the room and sat down on the floor beside Rose and Billy. He didn't look at Sarah. She could think what she wanted. And if Josiah wouldn't have done this, he didn't care either. He took a long piece of wool from the basket beside Florence and watched what the children were doing.

"How do you begin?" he asked.

Florence reached out and wound the wool around his fingers. Joe heard a sharp intake of breath. In spite of himself, he looked up. Sarah was gaping at Florence's hand touching his.

Suddenly, he'd had enough. "I can't do this,

Lucy!" he said. "I can't pretend like this." He was on his feet again.

Lucy looked up, alarmed.

"If your family can't accept me for who I am, just as you've done, then it's too bad."

"But …" Lucy began. "You can't just –"

"Be myself? Why not? Nobody wants Josiah back! Maybe they won't mind having someone else instead."

Lucy shot a look at Sarah. The young woman was watching with greedy interest.

"Let's go." Lucy stood up hurriedly. "See you later, Tommy."

Joe followed her out of the room. Her mouth was set in a thin line. When the door was closed, she shook her head at him. "That was not a good idea!" she said quietly.

"I'm sorry," Joe said. "I just couldn't stand it! Didn't you hear the way she was talking about Florence, in front of her? She's poisonous!"

"Maybe. But it's nothing to do with us."

"It felt like she was assuming we agreed with her!"

"I think perhaps Josiah did agree," Lucy said. "I know Tobias does. He doesn't trouble to hide it, even in front of my father."

"But your father thinks differently?"

"I'm not sure he knows what to think, but he did bring them back with him. In any case, you saying you're not Josiah in front of her, that could be really tricky."

"Only if she tells someone before I do."

"But you can't! Really, you can't! What did you think –" Lucy broke off. There were footsteps on the stairs, coming up towards them. They waited.

A head of dark, wavy hair appeared. From beneath it, a young man looked up.

Joe felt as though his heart clutched together in spasm.

"Ah, cousin Lucy," Tobias drawled. His gaze flicked across to Joe. "And Josiah! You haven't left us after all?" His eyebrows lifted, but his smile was one of genuine pleasure. It made his face quite handsome.

Joe's pulse raced. For the first time since he'd met Hannah, here was someone who was truly pleased to see him. But it was the last person in the world he wanted to please.

He bowed. "Tobias," he said. "As you see –" Just in time, he remembered the French accent. He straightened up and made himself smile back. "As you see, I am still 'ere."

120

10

"That is excellent!" Tobias beamed. "So you'll be able to see our little plan through, after all?" His eyes glittered. He jerked his head upwards.

Joe nodded.

"Good." Tobias disappeared through the door to the attics.

Lucy tugged Joe's sleeve. "What was that?" she mouthed.

Joe spread his palms.

She gestured to him to follow. Together they went down the two flights of stairs to the entrance hall, and through a door at the back which opened onto the garden. Outside, the air was still quite warm, with the fragrance of spring flowers.

Lucy led the way down to the end of the lawn. It wasn't a particularly large garden for the size of the house: Joe guessed you could see almost all of it from any of the back windows. He glanced up. Was Tobias watching them? The thought of it was enough to make the back of Joe's neck prickle.

It was only a few months since he'd last seen Tobias, but the other boy had changed a lot. He was taller now, and seemed much older somehow, a young man really, not a boy any more. Joe's stomach clenched. Tobias had always been bigger and stronger than him, but it would take even more courage to stand up to him now.

Lucy sat down on a bench beneath an arch of creepers. "We can't be overheard here," she said, speaking in a low voice nonetheless. "If we'd gone into my room or yours, Tobias could have listened at the door."

"What was he up to anyway?" Joe asked. "Didn't you say his room is on the first floor? Why was he going up to the attics?"

"I thought you knew," Lucy said.

"No, it just seemed best to pretend."

"Well, it sounds like he and Josiah had some sort of scheme." She bit her lip. "I can't imagine that was anything good."

"Do you think it's something to do with the footmen? They sleep up there, don't they?"

Lucy shook her head. "Tobias is much too self-important to have dealings with them."

"Amos, then?" Joe suggested.

"Maybe, though I can't see why Tobias would go looking for him either, instead of ringing the bell." She was quiet for a moment. "You know what this means, though, don't you?"

"What?"

"You absolutely have to carry on being Josiah. That way, you'll be able to find out what Tobias meant by your 'little plan'."

"How?" Joe exclaimed. "I can hardly say, 'By the way, Tobias, could you remind me what we were going to do? I seem to have forgotten.' "

Lucy ran her fingernail along the wood of the bench. "No. But you might be able to piece it together from what he says to you."

Joe sighed. "I suppose so. But if I have to carry on being Josiah, is there some way I can be a bit less awful? I can't bear it that everybody except Tobias hates me!"

"I don't hate you," Lucy said.

"No, of course you don't! But you know I'm not your cousin."

"So? That doesn't mean I'd necessarily like you." She sounded nettled.

"Sorry, that's not what I meant. It's just that we've been friends for so long, I assume you like me!"

"It hasn't been long for me! Only a few hours." She hunched her shoulders.

Joe was impatient. "That's another thing," he said. "If I manage to stay longer this time, what on earth do I do about going to school with Peter? You know I can't use a quill, and I've never done any Latin or Greek! I bet Josiah could do that stuff, so it's going to seem very peculiar that I can't."

Lucy pulled off a long tendril from the creeper and wound it through her fingers. Joe wondered if she was sulking over him taking her friendship for granted. But after a minute, she said, "It might not matter. Tomorrow is Sunday, so there's no school. And you were only here for just over half a day last time."

"That's true," Joe agreed. "All the same, we ought to have a plan."

"We could break your wrist!" Lucy teased. "That way, nobody could expect you to write." She laughed at the horror on Joe's face. "Don't worry, it won't come to that!"

"I should hope not!"

"In the meantime, you could pretend to my parents and Peter that you've had an epiphany."

"A what?"

"An epiphany. It's a message from God in a dream or something, like St. Paul on the road to Damascus. I mean, you already told my mother you'd taken the ship running aground as a sign that you shouldn't have left. You could build on that a bit, say God has told you to be nicer!"

Joe was thoughtful. "What about the French accent?" he asked. "I find it so hard to remember. And even when I do, it sounds totally fake. I can't believe I sound anything like Josiah!"

"You're right, it isn't very convincing." Lucy stood up from the bench and walked to and fro. "How about this?"

Joe listened as she explained. "Do you think they'll believe me?" he said doubtfully.

"Why not? It makes more sense than the truth, after all!"

"What about Sarah?" Joe asked. He was already regretting his earlier outburst.

"We just have to hope that either she forgets it, or she decides not to tell anyone."

Joe could hear that his friend didn't think either possibility was likely.

"Anyway, it's time to go in," she went on. "My father will be finishing work, and the children will come down to the withdrawing room to see my parents for a little while. My father likes us all to be there. That would be a good time for you to tell him what we just worked out."

As they walked back up the garden together, Joe gazed at the house. A man in a white wig sat at a desk behind the library window, busy over his papers. Joe felt sudden dread at the thought of meeting William. Lucy's father had always been generous and fair in the past, but Joe hadn't ever been impersonating someone he disliked.

Indoors, a fire burned in the withdrawing room grate, and some of the wall candles had been lit. Ellen sat near the fire talking to a woman Joe didn't know.

"Mother, Aunt Katherine," Lucy greeted them, with a curtsey. Joe bowed. Lucy's aunt gave him a fleeting smile, then looked away.

Joe took in the room. Above the mantelpiece was another circular mirror like the one in the parlour, reflecting a distorted image of the chandelier above him. He tipped his head back to look up. It was so immense, it seemed as though it might pull the ceiling down at any moment and bury him in glass. He stepped to one side, just in case.

Beneath his feet, a vast expanse of rug covered almost the whole floor, and there were more prim-looking chairs around the walls. Tobias slouched in the one nearest the door, making it plain he didn't want to be here.

Joe ducked his head as Sarah entered the room with Thomas in her arms. She set the baby down on the rug near Ellen's feet, and retreated. Florence came next, leading Rose and Billy to sit beside Thomas. Both children clung tightly to her, and even when she had got them to sit down, the girl would not let go. Florence knelt beside her and gently prised her fingers loose. When she had freed herself and rose to her feet however, the little boy jumped up and buried his face in her skirts. Florence glanced anxiously around. Joe saw Tobias' lip curl. From the doorway, Sarah sniffed.

"Thank you, Sarah," William said, entering the room with Peter close behind him. "Let me help you, Florence." He went over to the children and crouched down between Rose and Billy. Rose shrank away from him.

William put his hand on the small boy's shoulder. "Come along, little fellow. Would you like to play with my watch again?"

At once, Billy stopped sobbing.

"There now," said William, lifting him away from Florence and putting him on a couch. "That wasn't so bad, was it?" He smiled at their nursemaid. "They're getting better, don't you think?"

Florence nodded. For the first time, the wariness was gone from her face. "T'ere's a lot to forget, Massa," she said. "It take time to learn. Rose, she need more time t'an her brot'er."

Joe watched Rose cowering on the carpet, and wondered what had made her so fearful. He looked up to see what the others were thinking. Katherine's expression was anguished. Joe looked at Tobias. And his skin ran cold. Tobias knew what had been done to the girl, Joe felt certain.

William sat down beside Billy, who was immediately absorbed in opening and closing the case of a silver fob watch. Florence withdrew. Rose's gaze followed her. But when, after a few seconds, the door remained closed, she edged across the rug and began to play peek-a-boo with Thomas. Lucy dropped down to sit beside them, while Joe stood awkwardly, waiting for William to acknowledge his presence.

Lucy's father looked up. "So you've returned, Josiah," he said, without enthusiasm. Peter made a harrumphing noise. Joe's insides twisted. Out of the corner of his eye, he saw Lucy nod encouragingly.

"I have, Sir," he said, making no attempt to put on a French accent. "And I have a confession to make." The room fell completely silent. A candle sputtered.

Joe swallowed. Perhaps he should come out with the whole truth. Lucy had said not to, but maybe she was wrong. He hesitated. He could feel them all waiting. On the other hand, she knew better than he did how her family might react. He would be a fool not to take her advice.

"I can speak English like the rest of you," he said, finally. "My mother has always made sure I speak the same English she does."

"So why the accent all this time?" Peter snapped. "And why not now?"

Joe's throat rasped. He licked his lips. "It was my way of keeping myself apart from you all, remembering who I was."

"And making sure *we* didn't forget!" Lucy's brother glowered.

"Hush," said Ellen.

Joe continued. "I had a … " He tried to remember the word Lucy had used. Her lips were repeating it soundlessly, but he couldn't make it out. "I had a moment of realisation," he said, instead. "When the ship ran aground last night, I was dreaming I was ship-wrecked. I thought I was going to drown."

He heard Peter mutter something under his

breath.

"When I realised my life had been spared, I knew it was a sign that I should come back. I knew I must make amends for the way I'd behaved towards you all, be more civil and more honest with you." Joe cringed inwardly. Here he was, telling a pack of lies and claiming to be honest. "Please forgive me for the way I've been," he finished.

William stood up. "Of course we forgive you." He took Joe's hand and shook it. "I, too, have recently had my eyes opened to mistakes I've made. We shall both begin afresh as better people."

A choking noise came from Tobias. "This is nauseating!" He got to his feet, and banged out of the room.

William looked crestfallen. "For a few moments, we had the whole family assembled." His gaze encompassed all of the children. "Ah, well. We shall have to get on as best we can without Tobias." His eyes twinkled.

Joe sat down on the chair nearest to Lucy. His pulse was subsiding now, but he had no desire to say anything further to anyone. He also had the feeling that he might need to smooth things over with Tobias if he wanted to keep his trust. Distaste wrinkled inside Joe. He hated the thought of seeking Tobias' friendship, even in pretence.

For the next little while, he watched Lucy and Rose playing with Thomas, who gurgled in delight.

Family, he thought idly. William had said 'the whole family,' as if it included Rose and Billy. Joe looked at Rose. It was an odd sort of name for a child like her. Roses were usually creamy white or pink. Next to Lucy and Thomas, this child was distinctly dark, with jet black, curly hair. Yet beside Florence, she and Billy had looked quite light-skinned. Who were their parents, he wondered. Lucy had said something about a slave mother. But might she not be mistaken? Were they actually Katherine's children, by a black father? Was that why she seemed pained when she looked at them?

He was still puzzling over this when Sarah and Florence returned to take the children away.

"What do we do now?" he whispered to Lucy.

"We'll go back upstairs until supper time," she said. "I'm working on some embroidery. You can keep me company. You could bring a book from my father's library, if there's one that interests you."

Joe nodded. "Will you come with me to look?"

"No, you go on. I'll see you upstairs."

Joe had no choice. He wasn't at all sure there would be anything suitable. But if he didn't go and see, Lucy would think he was being cowardly, which he knew he was. He waited, in case William was going to resume work and give him the excuse not to go into the library. But Lucy's father had joined Ellen and Katherine by the fire. Joe went out quietly on his own.

It was dusky in the library after the brightness of

the withdrawing room. The fire had burned low, and the candles, which must have been lit earlier, were now extinguished. Joe browsed along the bookcase. A lot of the books seemed to be in Latin or French.

After a minute, he heard voices through the open door. On instinct, he moved down to the end of the bookcase and pressed himself flat against the wall, out of sight.

A man's voice sneered. "Not in there! The master's finished for the day. Don't waste candles on a room that no-one will use tonight, stupid nigger!"

Joe caught his breath. In his own time, that was a word racists used.

A second man spoke, just outside the door. "You're all the same, you lot. Lazy! Thick! Good for nothing!" He spat the words out. "They should round you all up, every nigger in England, and put you on a boat back to the West Indies where you belong!"

There was a sharp gasp, and then the first voice spoke again, sweetly this time. "Did I drip wax on your hand, Amos?"

For a moment, Joe thought he was about to apologise. Then the man went on, "Just trying to make your filthy black skin a bit whiter!"

There was sniggering laughter. "Imagine, if we covered you all over in burning wax, you'd be white like us! Except you wouldn't, would you, with the frizzy hair you're hiding under your wig and your flat nose! Was your nose always like that? Or did someone break it for you? We could break it again, and try and do better!"

Joe felt sick.

The laughter stopped abruptly as the withdrawing room door opened.

"Could we possibly have a little more light in here? Amos, would you oblige? Thank you, Jackson. Thank you, Metcalfe," William added curtly. "I'm sure Amos is capable of lighting such candles as we need without your help. Do attend to your other duties."

"Yes, Sir," simpered one footman.

"Of course, Sir," grovelled the other.

Joe held his breath, praying neither of them would decide to come into the library. But they pulled the door closed without looking in.

He waited until he was sure they'd gone, then took down a book at random and let himself quietly out. At the same moment, Amos emerged from the withdrawing room. Their eyes met. There was wordless fury in Amos' face.

Joe felt a rush of shame. Did Amos know he'd overheard? He should have done something to stop the footmen! But he hadn't.

Clutching the book tightly, he hurried up the stairs, head down.

"Steady on! Look where you're going!"

Joe drew up short. "Sorry."

"What's the big hurry?" Tobias asked. "In fact, never mind that, what was all that, down there?" His tone was unpleasant.

"You mean the footmen?" Joe felt a stab of panic. It would be bad enough if Amos realised he'd overheard. He definitely didn't want Tobias to know.

"What? No, this business of your grand realisation, and you not having a French accent. Is that true?"

Joe nodded.

"You might have let me in on the secret!" Tobias said. "I thought we were on the same side!" His eyes narrowed. "And what was all that about making amends?" He dropped his voice. "I hope you haven't changed your mind." It sounded more like a threat than a hope. "I don't want you going soft on me."

"No, no," Joe assured him quickly. "Not at all." He tried to guess what Tobias wanted him to say. "I just thought … if the rest of the family trusted me a bit more, it might be useful."

Tobias' eyebrows lifted slightly. "I see," he said. "An interesting tactic. Very well, don't forget to tell me if you have anything to report."

"Of course." Joe moved past him up the stairs, pretending to be calm. "The only problem is," he added silently, "I've no idea what it is you want to know."

11

Lucy was working at her embroidery. The curtains were drawn for the night, but a candlestick cast a pool of light across her lap. She looked up as Joe entered. "Did you find something to read? You were gone longer than I expected."

Joe told her about Tobias, and then about the footmen.

"Are you quite sure Jackson meant to spill the wax?" she asked, when he'd finished.

"I don't know which of them did it," Joe said, "but there's no question it was deliberate."

"It's bound to have been Jackson. Metcalfe never does anything without his say-so. Should we tell my father? Or do you think he knows?"

"I'm not sure. He might have realised something was going on, because he came out and sent the footmen away. Perhaps Amos will tell him." Even as he said it, Joe knew that wouldn't happen. Amos would probably think it was dishonourable to speak out.

The time until supper passed peacefully enough. Joe tried to read the book he'd brought upstairs. It was in English at least, entitled "A Treatise on Time". But he couldn't make head or tail of the first paragraph, never mind the first page. He soon gave up, and contented himself with watching Lucy's progress on her sampler until the gong rang.

The rest of the family were already gathered when Joe and Lucy went into the dining room. Only the little children were absent. Joe supposed it was much too late for them. The grandfather clock in the corner showed nine o'clock.

Supper was a lighter meal than the lunch they'd eaten last time he was here. But there were still three different dishes on the table as well as bread and cheese. The footmen stood to attention with their hands behind their backs, one beside the sideboard, the other behind William. Joe remembered what Lucy had said about their nickname. But after what had passed between them and Amos, he felt less inclined to laugh. Watching them now, so respectful and obedient, it was hard to believe what he'd heard through the library door.

William said Grace, and the family began to serve themselves. Jackson and Metcalfe buzzed around, needlessly passing the salt, pepper and vinegar, and filling glasses. For a time, everyone ate, and there was little conversation.

Then William said, "I was looking over the

accounts this afternoon. You know, the sugar boycott is really starting to have an effect." His brows were drawn together. "I thought perhaps it would fizzle out. But Wilberforce doesn't give up, and Clarkson and Fox are steadily winning people round. Parliament is debating the abolition of the Slave Trade again next week. In the meantime, they say three hundred thousand people have given up West Indian sugar." He contemplated the trifle on his spoon.

"Could you get your sugar from another source?" asked Ellen. "When I had tea with Mrs Carrington earlier this month, I couldn't help noticing that her sugar jar had text painted on it, saying that the sugar came from the East Indies and hadn't been grown by slaves."

William nodded. "I've made the initial enquiries. It will be long and complicated." He sighed. "After what I saw in Jamaica though, I'm beginning to think it's the only way."

"What utter rubbish!" Tobias exploded from the other end of the table. "There's no problem with using slaves to produce sugar! We think nothing of using horses to pull carts, or dogs to bring in the quarry when we hunt! Why is this any different?"

Joe's mouth fell open.

But William's reply was swift. "We're not talking about animals, Tobias! We're talking about people!"

"Hardly!" Tobias scoffed. "They're uncivilised savages! They can't read or write, they make noises that aren't proper language, they don't work unless you force them to, and you only have to look at them to see how close they are to apes!"

Joe held his breath. Beside him, Lucy looked at her father, her eyes wide.

William had turned pale. "Shame on you, boy! You've grown up among these people. I'd expect better of you!"

"Would you?" Tobias replied rudely. "It's *because* I've lived with them that I know what they're like! Whereas you visit for a few weeks and then have the nerve to think you know what's best for us all!"

Joe waited for William to roar at Tobias. But Lucy's father answered quietly. "Last year, when the bill to abolish the Slave Trade was rejected, I was glad," he said. "I'm ashamed to admit it now. But I was afraid of what abolition would do to my business.

"In my defence, however, I had never seen a slave. I knew the plantations were managed by slave labour, but I couldn't imagine the human cost. I should have tried harder, especially after I saw the print of the Brookes[*] slave ship. But I didn't want to hear what my conscience was telling me.

"You, on the other hand," his voice began to rise, "you don't have to imagine what it's like over there. You know! Your father's overseer was the most brutal man I've ever met! The state of your father's slaves was sickening!"

---

[*]   See page 229

137

"Barnard was just doing his job," growled Tobias. "You had no right to get rid of him! He was keeping the sugar coming for your sugar house, wasn't he? If you cared how much the slaves were fed or how they were treated, you could have paid more for the sugar! My father always said you expected special rates, just because you were family!"

William gave a bark of bitter laughter. "I did pay James special rates, well above the market rate, in fact!" he retorted. "He demanded more than I paid any of the other planters. And even if I'd paid ten times as much, the slaves wouldn't have seen a penny of it! It would just have been more money for my brother to drink and gamble away!" William shook his head. "He always was like that. That's why he was sent over there in the first place, to try and make something of himself!" He paused, then said, "You did know about the debts he's left?"

Tobias didn't reply.

"The plantation should have been quite profitable," William said, "despite the number of slaves he had to buy every year to replace the ones who'd died. But he owed money everywhere. The plantation will have to be sold to pay off his creditors. There's no alternative."

The room was suddenly still. All eyes were on Tobias.

The next second, he was on his feet. He thundered his fists on the table. His plate shot up. A glass fell over and shattered. His eyes blazed. "That's my inheritance!" he yelled. "You can't sell my inheritance!"

"Not just yours," William replied mildly. "It's your mother's too, as my brother's widow. And of course, there are Rose and Billy to think of as well."

Joe sensed Lucy's surprise.

"What?" Tobias' voice was a screech. "You can't count them as my father's heirs!"

"They're his children," William said with grim satisfaction. "I discovered that within a day of arriving over there." He glanced at Tobias' mother. "I'm sorry if I offend your sensibilities, Katherine. But it's high time this was talked about openly in the family."

"So what, that he fathered them?" Tobias shrieked. "They weren't the first! And they're still slaves like their mother. They have no claim on what's rightfully mine!"

"That may be true in strictly legal terms," William said. "But it's not a very Christian view, is it? These poor mites need someone to look after them. At least your father's other children still have their mothers. Billy and Rose's mother died in the fields, as you perfectly well know, carrying another of your father's offspring in her belly. That makes these children orphans. They have nobody but us."

Tobias spluttered.

"Of course," William went on, "once the debts are settled, there may be nothing left to divide between you in any case."

Tobias kicked his chair back so hard that it flew across the rug. The door slammed behind him.

Silence followed. At last, Ellen spoke. "Really, William. Was that strictly necessary?"

A muffled sob came from Katherine.

"There, there, my dear," William said, offering Lucy's aunt his handkerchief. "I know one shouldn't speak ill of the dead, but I'm sure we can agree that the world is a better place without my brother."

Katherine sniffed and nodded.

"We just have to hope we can steer your son in a different direction so he doesn't turn out like his father."

The rest of supper was a subdued affair. As soon as it was finished, Katherine went up to bed, Peter and William retired to the library, and Joe and Lucy sat politely in the withdrawing room with Ellen.

After a while, Joe excused himself and went upstairs, hoping Lucy would follow so they could talk in private. In Peter's room, the second bed had now been made up, with a bedspread over sheets and blankets. When Lucy didn't come, Joe undressed and took off his wig, putting on the nightshirt and cap which had been laid out for him. He climbed into bed.

It was more comfortable than he'd expected. He blew out the candle and lay in the darkness, thinking about the day. He didn't expect to fall asleep, since by his body clock it must be several hours earlier.

Nonetheless, he didn't hear Peter come in.

He was woken the following morning by the sound of someone moving quietly around the room. He opened his eyes to see Amos setting a jug on the washstand. Steam rose from it.

"Hello," he said sleepily.

Amos looked round, startled. "Good morning, Master Josiah," he said. "Here's water and soap for washing, and a cloth. I put you a toothbrush and some tooth whitener as well."

"Thank you, Amos."

From behind the drapes of the four poster, Peter groaned.

"Shall I open the curtains and shutters," Amos asked, "or leave them?"

"Could you open one side, just a little?" Joe asked. "Enough that I can see."

Amos did as he asked, and then left. Joe got up, washed and dressed, and picked up the little bristled brush. He unscrewed the lid of the jar beside it and peered down into it. The contents were black! How could that whiten the teeth? He decided to leave it until he'd had the chance to ask Lucy what was in it.

Breakfast was served in the dining room. Lucy, Ellen and Tobias were sitting at the table, attended as usual by the footmen, while they ate eggs and toasted bread with jam and marmalade. How wonderful, Joe thought! Not only was this the kind of breakfast he might have at home, but there was hot chocolate if he

141

didn't want coffee. When he tasted it, however, it was surprisingly bitter.

"You might want some sugar," Lucy said, with a grin.

At once one of the footmen sprang forward to pass Joe a bowl he could perfectly well have reached. He sipped again. Even with sugar, the chocolate didn't taste the same as it did at home. But it was still an enormous improvement on the beer that had been on offer in the past. He'd always found that especially hard to stomach in the mornings.

Tobias' thunderous presence was enough to keep Lucy and Ellen from talking. Joe took his seat beside Lucy, and they ate in silence.

When they arrived at church later, however, Tobias sat down beside Joe and leant towards him. "What would they all think?" he muttered, indicating the pews on the other side of the aisle. Joe waited for him to explain.

"It makes me sick! These men, they're the great and the good of the city! There's George Daubeny with his family, and Evan Baillie. And here's Sir Abraham Elton coming in now."

"Elton?" Joe repeated. That was another of the names Dad had mentioned.

"And here's the king pin of them all!" There was awe in Tobias' voice.

Joe watched a man make his way down the aisle, leaning on a cane. He was old enough that Joe would have thought him harmless, except perhaps for his supercilious expression.

"Thomas Daniel owns hundreds of slaves, maybe even a thousand! That's a man who knows what's good for business!" Tobias gazed with open admiration as the man passed the end of the pew and took his place at the front.

"And then there's our uncle, sitting among them like a cuckoo in the nest." Tobias shot a look of pure hatred towards William. "What would they say, if they'd heard the way he was talking last night?"

Joe nodded, hoping it looked like he agreed.

"I've half a mind to tell them!" Tobias carried on, with barely suppressed ferocity. "They would shun him! It would ruin his business!"

"I don't think that would be a good idea," Joe said. "Not just yet anyway," he added hastily. "Wait a while. If the plantation does have to be sold, you'll need our uncle not to be bankrupt."

Anger flashed in Tobias' eyes. "I won't let it be sold!" he snarled.

Joe was saved from replying by the organ falling silent. The vicar began to speak.

The service was very long, much longer than any church service Joe had ever been to in his own time. He let his thoughts wander and tried to stay awake. After about an hour and a half, his stomach started rumbling.

"You should have eaten more breakfast," Lucy

whispered.

Eventually, it was over and the congregation began to leave. Joe was tense, waiting for Tobias to approach the men he'd pointed out. But they reached the carriage without him uttering a word. Perhaps his own remarks had been enough to dissuade Tobias, Joe thought. Not for long, though.

Lunch, or dinner, as Lucy's family called it, was enormous and took up a good part of the afternoon. As at supper, the younger children were absent. Nobody mentioned the plantation, but the atmosphere of the previous evening hung over the table like a cloud.

Joe was grateful when it was over and Lucy suggested they go out to the garden. There was no chance of talking to her privately out there however, since Ellen and Katherine decided that they, too, would make the most of the warm spring weather. Worse, Sarah was outside already, sitting on a rug, throwing a small leather ball to Thomas.

She watched Joe and Lucy cross the lawn with a speculative look that made Joe squirm. He avoided her eye, praying that she wouldn't say anything about his outburst in the nursery. When he sat down beside Lucy, he was so distracted that he put his hand squarely on a streak of bird droppings. The slimy mess oozed between his fingers.

He jumped up. "I'll have to go and wash," he said to Lucy, and hurried back towards the house.

He was still in the powder room, drying his

144

hands, when he heard Tobias' voice in the hallway outside. He froze.

"Is that coffee for my uncle you've got there, boy?" Lucy's cousin asked smoothly.

"Yes, Sir," Amos' voice replied.

"It's 'Master' to you," Tobias corrected him. "The white man is your master."

Joe winced.

"Yes, Master." Amos sounded weary.

"Let me help you with the tray," Tobias offered.

Joe moved to peep through the crack in the door, wondering what Tobias was up to. All at once, the tray tipped violently. There was a crash. Shards of china scattered across the hall floor.

"Oh dear," crooned Tobias. "The idiot nigger has dropped the tray! And it's spilt coffee all down itself, too! Did you scald yourself, boy? I expect that hurt." He gave a high, unpleasant laugh. "Though of course, it's nothing to what you're used to!" He turned and went off up the stairs.

The library door opened. William looked down on Amos, who was now kneeling on the floor, collecting the broken china. "You really must be more careful, Amos," he said irritably. "I'm sure you know that it's caused a lot of discontent in the household, me bringing you here. This kind of thing only makes it worse."

Joe took a step towards the doorway of the powder room, then stopped. He waited for Amos to tell William what had happened.

But Amos' deep, beautiful voice said only, "I am sorry, Master. I promise it does not happen again."

"Very well. When you've finished clearing up and taken your shirt and cravat to be laundered, perhaps you could bring me some fresh coffee." The library door closed.

Indignation swelled inside Joe. Tobias couldn't be allowed to get away with that! He might have thought he was unobserved, but Joe had seen. He could tell William what Tobias had done!

And yet Amos had also had the chance to tell him, and had chosen not to. If he meant William not to know, what business of Joe's was it to interfere? He hesitated, still out of sight. Amos picked up the tray of smashed crockery and left.

Joe went out to the garden again, seething.

12

The rest of the afternoon passed slowly. Lucy was playing with Thomas when Joe came out again, so there was no chance of telling her what he'd witnessed. The injustice of it made his chest tight. Why hadn't Amos told William what had really happened? He shouldn't take the blame for something he hadn't done!

It was similar, in a way, to Jackson and the wax. Joe was quite certain now that Amos wouldn't have said anything to William about that either. Was it possible, he wondered, that Lucy was wrong and Tobias and the footmen were working together after all? But even if they were, he couldn't see what they hoped to achieve. Did they just want to make Amos' life miserable? Or did they have a more sinister goal in mind?

When at last he was alone with Lucy again, she brought up a different subject before he had a chance to mention it.

"Mother was talking about you going to school

tomorrow," she said, closing the door of her room. "You weren't sure you'd still be here, but since you are, we have to do something this evening – unless you've changed your mind about going with Peter?"

Joe gulped. He'd been so preoccupied with Amos, he'd forgotten all about school. "You're not still suggesting you break my wrist?" he asked, with a nervous laugh.

"I don't think so," Lucy said slowly.

"You don't think so!"

"It's just …" She frowned. "I can't think of any other excuse for you not being able to write. Maybe not a broken wrist, but it has to be an injury of some sort."

"An injury?" Joe echoed.

Lucy made a face. "It does really need to be something that stops you holding a quill."

"Couldn't we just pretend? What if I said I'd sprained my wrist?"

"What does that mean?"

"It's when you twist something awkwardly. We could bandage it up and put it in a sling."

Lucy shook her head. "Nobody will believe that. They'll think you're just making excuses for not going to school, which I suppose you are! I'm afraid it has to be much more convincing."

They were both quiet for a few moments. Then she said, "A cut across your writing hand would do it. It would have to be quite a bad one though, not just a

148

scratch."

"What with?" Joe asked faintly.

"We could use a penknife."

"But they're blunt!" he objected, thinking of his penknife at home.

"No, they're not!" Lucy stared at him. "You might have made a terrible job of cutting your quill, but it wasn't because the knife was blunt! Anything that cuts through the shaft of a goose feather is more than sharp enough for flesh."

They looked at each other. Joe shuddered.

"There *has* to be some other way!" he said desperately. "Couldn't I just lose Peter on the way to school and not turn up?"

"Not if you want to come back here at the end of the day," Lucy said.

"What if I told Peter the truth?" Joe said. "Then he could cover for me. I presume your parents are writing a letter for me to take, to explain why I'm back. The school won't be expecting me, so if I didn't turn up nobody would notice. As long as Peter knows the truth, that should work fine!"

"But you can't tell Peter you're not Josiah," Lucy insisted. "He won't believe you!"

"You did!" Joe was aware of his voice rising.

"I saw you vanish," Lucy reminded him, "and I still find it incredible."

She went over to the writing desk which stood beside the window. "Come on," she said, turning to

Joe. In her hand was a knife with a thin blade. "There's nothing else for it."

Joe backed away.

"Actually, wait a moment," Lucy said. "We'll need a cloth to wrap round the wound while we go and find my mother. We don't want blood everywhere." She went to the chest of drawers and took out a handkerchief which she spread on the desk. Then she motioned to Joe to come and sit down.

Haltingly, he crossed the room. He was still racking his brains for a way out of this. Perhaps he should just go to school with Peter and take the consequences. But he knew there would be no way of keeping up the pretence of being Josiah once he had failed to do everything Josiah could do.

A little cut on the hand wouldn't be so bad, he told himself. It was possible, of course, that the shock of doing it would spin him back into his own time. That would be annoying, but not disastrous. And it would have the advantage that he wouldn't have to put up with the pain for more than a few seconds.

The pain! He mustn't think about it! But his heart was pounding. He felt hot and shivery at the same time. His stomach had shrunk to nothing inside him.

He sank down in the chair in front of the desk. It was the deliberateness of it that was the problem, he reasoned. After all, he'd cut himself hundreds of times by accident, and it had never been a big deal.

"Can I see the blade?" he asked.

"You can hold it," Lucy replied. "You're doing this, not me."

Joe took the brass handle with trembling fingers. The blade was about as long as his thumb and as wide as the nail on his little finger. It looked viciously sharp, but at least it was clean as far as he could tell. He wiped it thoroughly on the handkerchief, just to be on the safe side. He knew he was procrastinating. He tested the cutting edge against his thumb. It was like a razor. His guts heaved at the thought of pressing it down through his skin.

Taking the knife in his left hand, he spread out his right, palm up. The blade quivered.

He screwed his eyes shut to summon up the courage, and thought about the scars he'd got in her previous worlds. Each of those wounds had been excruciating at the time. But they'd healed over the moment he was back in the present. So even if he cut through a muscle or tendon or something, it shouldn't matter. The trouble was, this time he might have to bear the pain for several days. Moreover, he hadn't known the other wounds were coming until they happened. He'd already had much too long to think about this one.

Beside him, he heard Lucy catch her breath. His eyes flew open. In the same instant, she seized the knife and slashed it across his hand.

Shock jolted through him. She'd said *he* had to

151

do it!

A scarlet line marked the path of the blade. He watched it broaden. He could barely feel anything, although blood was already spilling out of the cut. His heart hammered. Sweat broke out on his forehead.

Lucy was talking. He couldn't hear her properly. He saw a shape moving towards him. Then he couldn't see it any more. His mind swirled. Perhaps this was it. Perhaps he was slipping out of Lucy's time, though it didn't feel quite like it usually did.

Then she was bending over him. "Sorry, Joe," she said. "I saw that you couldn't do it." She wrapped the handkerchief tightly around his hand. At once, a bright red flower burst out over the cloth. "And then Aunt Katherine came in."

Joe turned his head, bewildered.

"It seems she can't stand the sight of blood." Lucy pointed to the floor. Katherine lay awkwardly, her skin ashen, her eyes closed. "It's probably just as well," Lucy went on. "I said you'd been cutting a new quill. But of course, there isn't one on the desk. If she hadn't fainted, she might have noticed. Here, hold this." She moved his left hand to pin the drenched handkerchief in place while she took out a quill and cutting board, and put them on the desk.

"Let's take you down to my mother, and get someone sent up to my aunt."

She helped Joe to his feet. He staggered. His head was still fuzzy and he felt nauseous. But he obviously wasn't going to be pulled back into his own world after all. He let Lucy steer him out of the room.

"Perhaps we should wash the cut," she suggested. And then almost immediately, "No, it'll look more impressive to my mother if you're really covered in blood."

They went slowly downstairs. Joe's limbs stopped shaking and his head cleared. His hand was now throbbing, but the reality of the pain was actually less bad than the thought of it.

He followed Lucy into the withdrawing room.

"Joe's cut himself," she said, without preamble.

Ellen looked up from her sewing. "It's Joe now, is it?" She raised an eyebrow.

Lucy reddened.

Her mother looked at Joe. "Dear me, what a mess!" She rang the bell. "Whatever were you doing?"

"Cutting a new quill for tomorrow, Aunt," Joe said. "The blade slipped."

"It really did!" Ellen looked at him quizzically. "Are you left-handed?"

Before he could reply, the maid appeared.

"It's not only Josiah who needs attention," Lucy said, taking care to get his name right this time. "My aunt fainted when she saw the blood. She's upstairs."

Swiftly, Ellen issued instructions for Mary to be sent to Katherine, and for Joe to go with the housemaid. Lucy didn't come with him.

At the door to the servants' staircase, Joe paused.

Lucy had said you didn't go down here. But the maid beckoned to him to follow. Downstairs, they went into a room with a scrubbed table, some sort of frame with wooden rollers, and a row of irons standing beside the fireplace. "Wait here please, Master Josiah," she said.

A minute later, she returned with a tray. On it were two bowls, one large and one small, a bundle of cloth and a jar of something yellowish. The maid began to tear the cloth into strips.

"Let's clean you up first," she said, unwinding the soaked handkerchief and dipping a piece of the cloth in the small bowl.

"Is that water?" Joe asked.

"That's right." The maid dabbed his hand gently. The water looked clean, and it was quite warm. Joe hoped that meant it had been boiled.

"There now. The bleeding has nearly stopped," she said. "Put your hand in here, and hold it under." She pushed the larger bowl towards him.

"What's that?" Joe was wary. This liquid was a clear brown colour.

"Brandy," said the maid. "It's just the thing for a wound."

"I'd rather not, if you don't mind," Joe said.

She looked taken aback. "Very well. In that case, we'll just put the balsam on." She unscrewed the lid of the jar. A smell rose up that reminded Joe of the time his parents had painted the kitchen.

"What is it?" he asked.

154

"Venice turpentine," she replied, smearing the grease across his cut before he could stop her.

"No!" Joe cried. Mum and Dad used turpentine to clean paint brushes! He snatched his hand away and started scrubbing at it.

"Now then, Master Josiah!" the maid exclaimed. "You need that to seal the wound."

"I don't want it," Joe said through gritted teeth, scouring it with a cloth. The cut started to bleed again.

"Now see what you've done!" The maid threw up her hands in dismay.

"I do not want that stuff on it!" he repeated. The pain made him gasp, but he carried on scrubbing. If it bled enough, the cut might wash itself clean.

"Alright, Master Josiah! Alright! Calm yourself! Let's bind it up then, nice and tight."

By the time Joe was back upstairs, the fingers on his right hand were purple from lack of circulation.

"All done?" Lucy asked.

"The maid just tried to put some horrible ointment on it," Joe snapped. He felt weak and sick. "It's one of the things I really hate about being with you – the so-called medicines and soaps and things. That reminds me, what was in the tooth stuff Amos gave me? Why was it black?"

"It's charcoal, of course, mixed with honey." Lucy sounded put out.

"Well, I suppose charcoal is better than the ashes of dogs' bones. But how could something black make your teeth whiter? This place is mad!"

Lucy glared at him. "I don't know why I bothered sorting things out for you! It would have served you right if you'd had to go to school with Peter after all!"

"But this was your bright idea!" Joe cried. "What did you have to 'sort out', apart from stabbing me!"

"My mother was convinced you were left-handed," Lucy said crossly. "She presumed you were holding the knife in your left hand to gash your right like that. She couldn't see why you'd have trouble writing!"

It made sense, Joe realised. "But you persuaded her?" He took a deep breath. "Thank you." He did his best to be contrite. "It would have been terrible to go through all this for nothing."

Lucy thrust her chin out. They set off up the stairs. Suddenly, she grinned. "You know what else she asked? She wanted to know if you really were so different since the ship."

Joe's eyes widened. "What did you say?"

"I said you were a changed person!"

They both laughed.

"Not too changed, I hope," came a voice from the landing above them.

Joe and Lucy looked at each other. Their laughter died on their lips.

"I rather liked the old Josiah," Tobias went on.

He was lounging in the doorway of his room. "What have you done to yourself?" he asked Joe, looking at the bandage.

"I cut myself with the penknife." Joe made himself look Tobias in the face.

"Oh dear," jeered Lucy's cousin. "You have to be so careful with knives." His attention shifted, to something or someone across the landing. "When a blade goes through flesh," he said, "it can do a lot of damage, can't it? Much more than coffee, say, or wax."

Joe's heart stopped. Amos must be up here.

"Some people are just careless once too often, aren't they, Josiah?" Tobias spoke deliberately. The threat was plain. Without waiting for Joe's answer, he sauntered off down the stairs.

"What was all that?" Lucy hissed, as they climbed the last few stairs to the landing. "Are *you* supposed to be more careful?"

"No." Joe jerked his head towards Amos, who was lighting the wall candles. The manservant's face was impassive, but the taper shook slightly as he put the flame to the next wick.

Joe moved quietly to stand beside Amos, more conscious than ever that he'd done nothing to defend him. The black man stood completely still.

"Were you hurt?" he asked in a low voice. It was cowardly, he knew, but he didn't want Tobias to overhear him. "The wax yesterday and the coffee this afternoon – did they hurt you?"

Amos didn't look at him. "What do you think, Master Josiah?" he replied, without emotion.

"Why didn't you tell William, then? Why didn't you say Tobias knocked the tray out of your hands?"

Amos stretched his arm towards the next candle. The taper was steady now. "You are Master Tobias' friend, no?" he said, without looking round.

"No, I'm not. I know why you think that. But believe me, I hate him as much as you do."

A sound came from Amos that was almost a chuckle. "I beg your pardon, but that is not possible." He was silent again. Joe wondered if he was waiting for them to go away. Then Amos said, "He is the master. I am the slave."

"Tobias isn't your master," Lucy corrected him. "And you're a servant, not a slave. You should stand up to him!"

Amos turned. There was a glint of humour in his eyes. "Just as you would stand up to your father? Refuse to do his bidding? That is not the way of the world, Miss Lucy. We both know it."

He blew out the taper and stood looking at the flames burning above their heads.

"Master Tobias is one of you," he went on, "just as Mistress Katherine is one of you, and your own father and mother and brother. You are all the same."

"No, we're not!" Lucy said hotly.

Amos smiled at her. "Not quite, perhaps. But I must do as each of you bids me. That is my place in

158

the world." He turned to Joe. "Of course my skin burns and bleeds like yours does. I feel rage when I am badly treated, and frustration. But I have learned to hold my tongue. I can bear more pain, more hatred and anger, than you will ever know. A slave who cannot do that cannot survive."

There was another silence.

"It's not like that here though, is it?" Lucy asked in a small voice. Her face was white.

"The work is easier," Amos answered. "There is more food, I am more comfortable and not often afraid. I haven't been whipped since we left Jamaica, so the sores on my back are closing up at last." He gave a wry smile at the children's appalled faces. "Your father is a kind master, Miss Lucy, unlike his brother. But he still owns me. I am still his slave. And there is not a day when the servants let me forget that."

He lit the taper again and climbed the next flight of stairs to continue lighting the candles further up.

Joe and Lucy stood side by side and watched him go. Neither of them spoke. They didn't know what to say.

13

Monday and Tuesday crawled by. Joe's lessons with Lucy started straight after breakfast and went on until five o'clock. As before, they took it in turns to read from the Bible, but other than that, Joe mostly just watched. Miss Waters didn't suggest painting again, presumably because of Josiah's catastrophic art lesson. But in any case, Joe couldn't have held a paintbrush. He'd loosened the bandage around his hand the evening it had been put on, and it definitely hurt less now, so the cut couldn't have got infected, despite what the maid had tried to put on. All the same, he didn't dare take the dressing off.

The one lesson he did enjoy was maths. Lucy was learning arithmetic for doing household accounts, and since Joe had always been good at quick maths, he could work out the answers faster than she could, even though she had an abacus to help her.

At mealtimes, he kept quiet, and he avoided Tobias as much as possible, taking care not to bump into him on the stairs. As it happened, he and Lucy saw very little of Amos either, and only saw Florence when she brought Rose and Billy down to the withdrawing room each evening. Sarah brought Thomas at the same time, but Joe made sure he didn't catch her eye.

It did feel as though he and Lucy had very little free time compared to when he'd first arrived. So he was pleased when after dinner on Wednesday, Lucy suggested they go out for a walk.

"Miss Waters gives me the afternoon off every other week," she explained. "Shall we go down to the quay or up to the park at the Royal Fort?"

Hearing her, Lucy's mother said, "I'd rather you didn't go down to the quay. Your father said there's been trouble down there. I wouldn't want you to get caught up in a fight."

"What's happened?"

"It's just the *Isabella*, preparing to sail. Captain Roper is one of the rougher sort, and he always finds reasons not to pay his crew. It's well known among the sailors. Sometimes, the only way he can get a crew together is to have men tricked into signing up."

"How?" Joe asked.

Ellen shrugged. "Bets at cards, I think, and crimping – they slip a shilling into a man's beer. If he drinks from the tankard, they say he's agreed to serve the king, which means going to sea.

"Anyway, no man who's sailed with Roper

before wants to do it again. So the fighting will probably carry on until the *Isabella* leaves port."

"We'll go up to the Royal Fort, then," Lucy said. "It's a beautiful afternoon."

It was. The sky was bright blue as they left the house. But a sudden shower soaked them as they were crossing the park, and they got wet again on the way down. Joe's hat kept the worst of the rain off, though water still dribbled down inside his collar where the damp ponytail of his wig lay against his neck.

As they approached the house, they saw Florence coming from the other direction with Rose and Billy. All three had the hoods of their cloaks drawn up. Joe wondered why, since the rain had stopped. Then he noticed a woman on the other side of the road staring at them. From the scaffolding of one of the houses behind Joe and Lucy came jeering and shouting obviously aimed at Florence.

He was about to comment on this to Lucy when they saw Florence stop dead in front of the house. Her hand flew to her mouth to stifle a cry. She drew the children close to her, then opened the gate in the railings and hustled them awkwardly down the steps. She seemed to be trying to keep herself between them and something she'd seen below.

Joe and Lucy hurried down the street until they came to the railings. In the cramped yard beneath, Jackson and Metcalfe had pinned Amos to the wall. One of Amos' eyes was swollen shut and his head sagged. They were thumping and kicking him.

"Wake up, boy!" Jackson sneered, hitting Amos hard across the face. "The fun's not over yet!"

He nodded to Metcalfe, who slammed his knee into Amos' groin. The black man groaned. Jackson buried his fist in his stomach. Amos doubled over.

"Stop!" Lucy cried. "Stop!"

The footmen looked up. Metcalfe's fist was raised for the next blow. Jackson's face flushed angrily.

Amos opened one eye. Blood was caked beneath his nose and trickled from the corner of his mouth. His cravat was already spattered with scarlet drops. He, too, looked up at Joe and Lucy. For a long moment, he held Joe's gaze.

Then he pulled himself upright. Slowly, painfully, he drew back his arm. And punched Jackson full in the face.

Jackson stumbled. He clutched his nose and swore. Metcalfe stepped hastily back. Amos slumped down.

"You see, Miss Lucy," whined Metcalfe. "He's a savage! They all are! They'll rise up and kill us in our beds unless we keep them under control!"

Jackson was on his feet again. "You have to teach them who's master!" he snarled. Blood was now running from his nose, too. "Trouble, is, some niggers just won't learn!" He gave Amos a hefty kick, then turned and stomped into the house, followed by Metcalfe.

For a second, Joe and Lucy stood stunned. Then Joe ran down the steps. He knelt beside Amos, who lay in a heap against the wall.

"Can you hear me?" he asked. There was a flicker from Amos' good eye. "That was brave!" Joe squeezed Amos' arm. The black man flinched. Joe let go quickly. Amos looked somehow more beaten and defeated than before he'd hit Jackson.

His lips moved.

"What did you say?" Joe bent close.

"Stupid," Amos mumbled. A moan of pain escaped him. "Stupid nigger."

"Don't say that! Don't use that word!" Joe glanced round. Lucy was still at the top of the stairs. "Come on!" he called. "We need to get him inside."

Lucy didn't move.

"Come on, Lucy!" Joe was impatient. "I know the footmen are in there, but I don't know what else we can do."

"I'm not sure … I don't know …" She clutched the railing. "I've never been down there."

"Well, there's a first time for everything," Joe said sarcastically. "The steps seem to be like any other steps, and I expect the door opens like any other door."

As if in answer, the door swung open. Joe whipped round. Surely Jackson and Metcalfe weren't coming back for more!

But it was Florence. She paused, flustered at the sight of Joe beside Amos, then rushed across the yard.

"Leave him, Massa Josiah! I do it!" She fell to her knees and cupped Amos' chin in her hand. His blood smeared red across her palm. "Foolish!" she wept. "Foolish!" She took out her handkerchief and began to clean his face gently, murmuring words Joe couldn't understand. Amos replied to her. Then he opened his eye again. "Go, Master Josiah," he said, in English. "You have done enough."

"But I haven't done anything!" Joe protested.

"You and Miss Lucy, you made me remember who I once was." A smile flickered across Amos' battered face. But his voice was sad. "Now you will see what happens to a slave who forgets his place."

Florence broke into a gale of sobbing.

Reluctantly, Joe stepped back. He wasn't sure that the footmen would have stopped before they'd killed Amos. And it had been so satisfying to see him repay just a little of their cruelty! But perhaps he and Lucy had somehow encouraged Amos into much greater trouble. He quailed at the thought.

By the time they went down to the withdrawing room at six o'clock, Joe was sick with worry. So he was horrified to find all the servants gathered at one end of the room. Ellen, Katherine and Peter were seated at the other end. Everyone was waiting for William to arrive.

Joe scanned the group. There was Hannah, who he hadn't seen since the first day, as well as Mary, Morley, and the housemaid who'd bandaged his cut.

There was no sign of Amos or Florence, nor were the children present this evening, although Sarah stood beside the housemaid, her eyes bright with anticipation. In the centre of the group were the two footmen, plainly enjoying their new celebrity. Metcalfe's arm was in a sling, for no reason as far as Joe knew, and Jackson's nose was puffy and an odd, greenish colour. Joe hoped it was broken.

The servants fell silent as Tobias entered the room, followed by William. Tobias' eyes met Jackson's. Joe was sure that something passed wordlessly between them.

William went to stand beside the mantelpiece. For a few moments, he looked at the group of servants.

"Thank you all for leaving your tasks," he said, at last. "I am well aware that I have put this household under strain by bringing four of my brother's slaves back from the West Indies. Several of you have been displaced, several have more work to do. For all of you, as for the family, there has been an adjustment to living alongside people who look so different to ourselves. Many of you have no doubt wondered why I did it. Indeed, it's a question I ask myself every day. Why bring these four when there were over a hundred others I might equally have brought?"

He looked around again. "The answer is simple: I couldn't bring them all. So why not leave these four? What is the good of bringing so few? I can only remind you of the words of Edmund Burke: nobody

166

made a greater mistake than he who did nothing because he could only do a little."

There was shuffling of feet amongst the servants. William waited for them to be still, before continuing. "What I am trying to do is to compensate in my own small way for what our country, and our countrymen, have been doing to innocent people; what this city, and sugar houses like mine, are doing to men, women and children every day."

The room was completely quiet. Even Tobias was silent, though his face showed contempt.

"I haven't seen the very worst," William said, "the galleys of the ships where the slaves are crowded together in darkness, closer than you stand, shackled to each other. But I've stood on the quayside watching just such a ship approach after months at sea, and I have smelled the stench carried on the wind. You cannot imagine a fouler smell!

"A doctor I met told me how he had to go aboard the ship, and try to make the slaves look healthy before any buyer could see them – how their sores were covered with iron rust and gunpowder, and rum was dropped into their eyes. Those suffering from the flux were subjected to the indignity of a cork to prevent blood and faeces from leaking out. When this was done, they were made to jump and dance to show how fit they were, though many were so sick and starved, they were little more than skeletons."

Joe found he was scarcely breathing. Beside

him, Lucy was pale.

William went on, "I was told that one in ten slaves dies on the ship before it even reaches the West Indies. Another three will die of tropical diseases in the first three years. The remaining six will suffer from malnourishment, exhaustion, and brutal punishments for the smallest mistakes. I heard of hands cut off, ears nailed to trees, hot ashes rubbed into the open wounds made by the whips of the slave drivers and plantation managers."

His eyes swept the room. "I can see from your faces that many of you wish I wouldn't talk of this. But I must, if I am to win your sympathy for those who have known such horror, most especially when it has been inflicted by our fellow Englishmen, even my own brother."

He looked down at his palms.

"Four of these people are under this roof," he went on quietly, "and it has come to my attention that not everyone in this room has been treating them with decency and respect." William let his gaze travel over the servants without settling on any individual.

When he spoke again, there was an edge to his tone. "I wish to make it clear that no matter what, I shall not send any of the four away. This house is their refuge."

Joe stole a look at Jackson. There was unconcealed outrage in his face.

"Therefore, if any person here -" William paused

for several seconds. "If any servant feels unable to live in harmony with Amos, Florence, Rose and Billy, they should immediately seek a position elsewhere."

There was a shocked silence.

"Very well." William took a step backwards. "Sarah," he said. The nursemaid started visibly, and blushed. "We won't have the children down here this evening. I've told Florence so already. If anyone wishes to speak to me, I shall be in my study."

Frantic whispering broke out among the servants the second he had gone, continuing unabated as Tobias stalked out, followed by Ellen and Katherine, and then Peter. Joe and Lucy stayed in their chairs till all the servants had left. Even then, they didn't speak. Joe watched the flames leaping in the fireplace and thought about what Amos and Florence must have endured. He understood better now why Rose might be so afraid. And he hated Tobias more than ever for defending such a thing.

Tobias was the last member of the family to enter the dining room for supper later on. He halted just inside the doorway. "Where are the footmen?" he asked sharply, seeing Morley at the sideboard.

"Gone." William's face was grim. "As expected, they saw it as an affront to their dignity that I refused to dismiss Amos."

"I don't wonder at it!" Tobias blew up. "It's a disgrace! You give a black man shelter out of some misplaced sense of obligation, and when he shows his

169

gratitude by breaking a white man's nose, it's the white man who has to leave!"

"Have you seen Amos?" William growled. His eyes burned. "It's evident from his injuries that he was provoked. And not just today! He seems to have burns and cuts all over the place, all of them fresh!"

Tobias snorted. "You're just weak and sentimental! In Jamaica, he would have paid for this with his life!"

William sprang to his feet. "This is not Jamaica! Moreover, this is *my* house, where *I* am master. *I* shall decide how to administer justice. And I will not be lectured by you!"

Tobias turned on his heel and marched out of the room.

William was stony-faced for the rest of the meal. Nobody dared speak, and Joe was glad when it was over and they could go up to bed.

Tension lay heavily over the house all the next day. The servants, who were always quiet, were now entirely silent. Joe was woken by a boy he didn't know opening the shutters. He wondered where Amos was. Recovering, he hoped. He hardly dared think what damage the footmen might have inflicted. Even if Amos' bones were intact, something might well be ruptured inside. But nobody would be able to find that out or treat it in this world.

And what about Florence? Did she know what had been said last night, he wondered, as he watched her shepherd Rose and Billy into the withdrawing room at six o'clock that evening. She looked anxious, but then, she always did, so it was hard to tell.

Sarah came into the room behind her, carrying Thomas. "Come and play with dear Rose and Billy," she said, in a sickly sweet voice.

Florence was still trying to free herself from Rose's grasp.

"Let me help you," Sarah cooed. "Rose, could you hold Thomas for me? I'm sure he'd like to sit on your lap."

Joe wondered what had come over her.

Rose peeped out from behind Florence, her eyes as fearful as ever. Sarah held Thomas out. He gurgled and reached towards the girl, who hesitated and then took him in her arms. Sarah's smile became wooden, as though she was stifling some other reaction. But she managed to thank Rose.

"Could you stay for a few minutes, Sarah?" Ellen said.

Sarah straightened up. Her eyes flicked from left to right. She curtseyed.

Florence left. Ellen nudged her husband, who was fiddling absent-mindedly with the fob watch he sometimes gave Billy to play with.

"Ah yes, thank you, Sarah," he said vaguely, his thoughts still elsewhere. Joe wondered if it was anything to do with Tobias or Katherine, neither of whom were present today.

William gave a cough. "You'll be aware there have been some changes in the household since this time yesterday," he said. "As well as our footmen, who were frankly dispensable -"

"Good riddance!" muttered Peter.

"- we have lost our housemaid, who was not."

Sarah nodded. "Rachel was sweet on Jackson, Sir. She didn't want to stay without him."

"That's as may be. The point is, we now have two nursemaids when we only need one, and no housemaid."

The muscles in Sarah's face tightened. But she said levelly, "I'll be very happy to look after Billy and Rose so that Florence can be trained up."

Ellen shifted in her chair. "Naturally, we have considered that possibility," she said. "However, we feel that Rose and Billy have suffered such upheaval in the last few months, they need the stability of Florence's care. The better solution, therefore -"

"- is for me to be reduced to housemaid!" Sarah burst out. The bitterness in her voice was unmistakable.

She rounded on Joe. "This is *your* fault!" she shrieked. "You told them I said Florence should be sent back to the plantations!"

Before Joe could protest, she spun to face William. "You don't want to believe anything that boy tells you, Sir! He isn't who he says he is! He's not Miss Lucy's cousin at all. If you don't believe me, ask her!"

There was a moment of astonished silence.

Ellen sat forward. "What do you mean?"

Sarah looked at Joe through eyes like slits. "The day after Master Josiah left – the real Master Josiah – the day he supposedly came back, they came into the nursery, him and Miss Lucy." She jerked her head towards Joe. "I knew at once something was wrong. Miss Lucy was too friendly with him for one thing. Did you ever see them together before?" She pressed her lips together in satisfaction. "Then he got down on the floor with the Negro children and Florence. Not that there's anything wrong with that," she added hurriedly. "But Master Josiah wouldn't have done it, would he?" She stopped to enjoy the effect her speech was having on her listeners.

"And then -" another dramatic pause "- he actually admitted it! As true as I'm standing here before you! 'I can't pretend like this,' he says. 'Nobody wants Josiah back! Maybe they won't mind having someone else instead.' " She shot Joe a look of absolute malice.

There was another silence. Joe wished the floor would open up beneath him.

Finally, William spoke. "What do you have to say to this, Josiah? And if you're not Josiah, whoever are you?"

14

Joe and Lucy both answered at the same time.

"It's true," Joe said.

"She's lying!" Lucy declared.

They exchanged looks. Joe held up his bandaged hand. "No, Lucy," he said. His heart was pounding. "This has gone on long enough. It is true," he repeated, looking William in the eye. "I'm not Josiah."

"But you look so like him! How is this possible?" Ellen scrutinised Joe. "Though now I think of it," she went on, "you do lack certain mannerisms. In fact, your demeanour is quite different." She said something in French.

Joe gazed at her blankly.

She shook her head. "You really didn't understand what I just said, did you? I asked about your hand."

"Oh. I see. We did it deliberately," Joe said. "It was supposed to me, but I couldn't do it, and then Lucy did it, because we realised I couldn't go to school

174

with Peter." He knew he was babbling. He'd dreaded this moment. But now it was here, it was a relief to get it all out. "I wouldn't have been able to do any of the work, you see. Where I come from, we learn different things."

He trailed off, watching Lucy's mother. She seemed intrigued rather than angry. Perhaps it would all be okay. Maybe they would let him stay.

But then William spoke, his voice hard. "So your grand confession," he said, "this revelation that you should be more honest with us – it was a lie!"

Joe hung his head.

"And the business of the French accent?"

"I'm not French," Joe said miserably.

"I see. And you're not my nephew either! Which begs the question, who *are* you?"

Joe looked imploringly at Lucy. She was staring down at her lap, her face taut.

"I'm -" He floundered. He wanted to be truthful. But Lucy had been confident that none of them would believe him. The seconds stretched out.

"My name is Joe," he said at last. "Short for Joseph, actually. When I first arrived in Bristol, and Hannah saw me, I didn't realise she'd mistaken me for Josiah. I went along with it because I had nowhere else to go."

"So it was you who arrived that morning in February!" Ellen said. "And then the real Josiah appeared – when? Later that day? That explains a lot," she added to herself. "And where did you go when he arrived?"

Joe swallowed. "I disappeared." He strained his ears, hoping against hope to hear the telltale hissing. Everything would be so much easier if he vanished back into his own world right now. If Lucy's parents saw it, they would understand in a way he could never explain.

But there was no hiss. He remained solidly in the withdrawing room.

"You disappeared," William repeated coldly. "You turned up, a perfect stranger. You took advantage of our hospitality. You pretended to be someone you weren't. And when the real boy appeared, you just went!" He spat out the last two words. "How convenient for you that Josiah decided to leave us last week! All that nonsense about the ship going aground, it was one lie after another!"

Joe looked at the floor.

"Leave now!" commanded William.

"But, father," Lucy cried out, "he couldn't help it! And he's kinder and more decent than Josiah ever was!"

"That is neither here nor there!" her father snapped. "I cannot have someone in my house who has duped us all. How could we trust him now?"

"Please!" Lucy begged. "I know him. I trust him!"

Joe stood with his head bowed, awaiting

sentence.

"I have problems enough without this, Lucy." William stood up. "Joe – Joseph – whoever you are, wherever you came from, go now!"

Joe raised his head. "I'm sorry," he said to Ellen. Then he turned to William. "I didn't mean any harm."

He glanced at his friend. Her eyes were bright with tears. He couldn't say goodbye to her here, not in front of the others. Avoiding Sarah's gaze, he left the room.

In the hall, Morley had his hat and coat ready. Joe took them meekly. He looked around for some way to delay. But he had nothing to pack, and he was wearing the clothes he'd arrived in. There was nothing to stop him leaving right now.

Still he wavered. He didn't want to go without saying goodbye to Lucy. But she didn't come out.

He waited another minute, conscious of Morley standing expectantly by the front door. Joe imagined himself still here when William emerged. He gulped. Better to go now. Perhaps he might see Lucy later somehow, or tomorrow.

The front door closed instantly behind him. Standing on the doorstep, Joe looked up and down the street. Where could he go? The evening was cool. He put on his coat and hat. If the temperature dropped overnight … He shivered. Was he really going to sleep in a doorway, or under a hedge? Perhaps he should try one of the half-built houses. At least he might find shelter there. He trotted down the steps and set off up the road.

On the corner of the street that led to Brandon Hill, he paused. No noise was coming from the building site. He walked up the track towards it. The workmen seemed to have left for the day. Joe tried to take heart from this. They might easily have still been there, since it wasn't yet dusk.

He approached the two unfinished buildings at the end of the track. They stood silent and unlit. There was glass in the windows of the first, but when Joe tried the door, it seemed to be barred. He stepped back. The rooms behind the glass were empty, so there was nothing to steal. But perhaps other people might have had the same idea as him. A house like this could be taken over by whole families at night if it wasn't shut up.

He turned to the other unfinished building. The windows of this one were empty, like eye sockets in a skull. He moved closer and listened. No sound came from within. All he could hear were the distant cries of seagulls from the quay, and the occasional shout over the rumbling of wheels.

Quietly, he walked round to the back of the house until he found a window he could reach. He listened again. Nothing. He climbed awkwardly onto the sill, careful not to rip his breeches or snag his coat or stockings. Not that it mattered, he thought. After all, there was nobody but him to care. A wave of loneliness swept over him.

He swung his legs over the sill and dropped down onto the floor. Inside the walls, the sounds of the city were even fainter. He wandered through the rooms until he found a dry corner that wasn't too draughty. With no idea of what else to do, he huddled down.

In a few minutes, a chill had seeped right through him. The floor was wood but the walls were stone. He turned up his collar and tried sitting forward. It was less cold but just as uncomfortable. He wondered if he might be able to sleep. It would be better if he could. He would have to be gone at dawn, before the workmen came back.

But it was too early. Sleep didn't come. Instead, he sat wretchedly, with his chin on his knees, wondering what on earth he was going to do.

He must have dozed without realising, however, because he was startled into alertness by voices. He rubbed his eyes. It was dark now, except for the glow of a lamp beyond the doorway to the next room. Two men were talking quietly. They must have sought shelter here like him.

He was so cold now, his muscles felt stiff. He breathed on his hands to warm them. Then he heard something that made his heart stop.

"Joseph something or another," one of the voices said, "not Josiah. So he said, anyway. In any case, my uncle sent him packing. I wish I'd been there!"

The other person mumbled agreement.

Joe's heart started beating again, extra fast as though it wanted to leap out of his chest. The first voice had to be Tobias. But who was he talking to?

"You know, I was wondering what was the matter with him," Lucy's cousin went on. "He was different to before. He was supposed to be doing his bit, same as you and me. But I didn't see it once after he came back."

The other voice spoke. "Can we make something of it, do you think?"

Joe shut his eyes to listen. He knew this voice. But it didn't usually speak like this. This was a voice that whined or jeered.

"Maybe." Tobias was thoughtful. "We could make it look like he lured them away, as revenge on my uncle."

"What would we do? I thought the plan was to get them to leave of their own accord?"

Tobias gave a short laugh. "I'd already given up on that! After all, you had a good go, and see where that got us! No, I've been thinking, we can do better than that, if you're still willing to lend a hand. I reckon there's money to be made."

"You think? Well, I'd not say no, though the nigger did me a favour actually. Old Daniel's paying me more than I was earning before, and there's a chance of advancement. Even without that, it's good to be back in a house where we all think alike."

Joe held his breath. This must be Jackson.

180

"Alright for some!" Tobias grumbled. "But I haven't given up. I was asking around today. There's a man who collects runaway slaves. Someone said he sells them back to the plantations. He's bound to have contacts in the West Indies. If we can get our four on the *Isabella* when it sails, we should make a tidy sum."

"But is the nigger fit enough?" Jackson asked. "I gave him a lot worse than he gave me!" There was a note of pride in the footman's voice.

"I don't care if he's fit or not!"

"I was only thinking of the price," wheedled Jackson. "We'll get more for him if he looks well."

There was a pause. Then Tobias said, "We could take them tomorrow, so that it looks like the boy's revenge, then keep them somewhere till the nigger's face has healed."

He stopped, then went on, thinking aloud. "The *Isabella* might leave any time, mind you. Once it's gone, we could have a long wait for the next ship. It might be better to say there was a scuffle when we took him. The others will be in better shape if we hand them over straight away, too. And trying to hide them will be risky. My uncle will have search parties out the moment they're missed, and I'm not sure where we could keep them that they wouldn't be found."

In the next room, Joe struggled to his feet, trying not to make a sound. Tobias and Jackson had relaxed enough to talk normally, but they would still notice any unexpected noise. He squinted around in the darkness. There was only one doorway, and they were on the other side of it. But there was a window. He could climb out of that. Then he could get back to Lucy's house and warn her and her father.

He clambered onto the sill as quietly as he could and peered down outside. But the drop from this window was much further than he'd expected, three metres at least! This room must be above the servants' entrance. He swallowed and screwed up his eyes to try and see better. The ground below looked uneven and rocky. If he jumped, he might well break his ankle.

Suddenly, lamplight swung across the room. Joe froze. Shadows sprang through the doorway and loomed on the walls. He crouched in the window, still as a stone, praying Tobias wouldn't notice him.

But it was a vain hope.

"Well, well! Look, Jackson! I did hear something. It's the imposter himself!"

The two young men advanced on Joe. He scanned the ground outside again. But there was nowhere he could safely land. As he swivelled round, Jackson flew at him.

"You see this?" He jabbed at his broken nose. "This is your fault!"

"Mine?" Joe faltered. "But Amos –"

Jackson didn't let him finish. He grabbed Joe by the shoulders and hauled him down from the sill. Tobias stood back, watching.

"It was you the nigger was looking at before he

punched me!" Jackson screeched. "The thought hadn't crossed his mind until you came along with that snivelling little girl!"

Joe shook Jackson's hands off him, abruptly furious. "How dare you call Lucy snivelling! When I think how you crawled to your master! 'Yes, Sir! No, Sir! Three bags full, Sir!' " he mimicked.

Tobias sniggered. Jackson's face darkened.

"You encouraged a black man to rise up against his betters!" the footman roared.

Joe knew he should be afraid. It was two against one, and they were both a good deal bigger than him. But rage made him feel invincible.

"What makes you better than Amos?" he yelled back. "I know what you were doing, even before you beat him up. I know what you did with the wax, and you –" He rounded on Tobias. "I know what you did with the coffee. But Amos was man enough to take your bullying and say nothing! He's tougher than you, and he's braver too!"

The smirk was gone from Tobias' lips.

Joe thundered on. "You think because you have white skin, and his is black, that you're better than him! Well, you're not! He's more of a man than both of you put together!"

He stopped to draw breath. He hadn't expected to get this far before one of them attacked him. His eyes flicked from Tobias to Jackson, and back to Tobias again.

But it was Jackson who lunged. Joe darted sideways beneath his fist. The footman staggered, then straightened up, ready to swing again. This time, Joe's way was blocked by Tobias.

"A real nigger lover, aren't you?" Tobias sneered. "You're even worse than my uncle! Such a pity you won't be able to save them! I expect that's what you were thinking, you little rat! But we've got you now. We'll finish you!"

Joe saw the pleasure in Tobias' eyes.

"And you know the best thing of all? Nobody will even miss you!"

Joe weighed his options swiftly. It sounded as though Tobias was prepared to kill him. Fear ran through Joe's blood. But Tobias wouldn't be able to do it, he reminded himself. He was almost sure to be pulled back into his own world.

If that happened though, he wouldn't have the chance to warn Lucy. Tobias and Jackson would kidnap Amos and the others, and sell them back to the slave traders. For their sake, he had to try and escape!

He ducked Jackson's second punch and flung himself towards the door.

It was futile, he knew at once. Tobias whipped round and caught him with a massive blow to the stomach. Joe keeled over, unable to breathe.

His attackers closed in, kicking and pounding him as he lay on the floor. Joe curled his arms around his head. His knees were up by his stomach. It didn't seem to help. The assault came from all sides, one crunching blow after another.

On and on it went, or so it seemed. Was this how Amos had felt, Joe wondered, waiting for the end? For Amos, of course, the only end would be death. Perhaps this was what death was like, the fading of pain into the distance. In fact, perhaps this *was* death, Joe thought. Perhaps *he* was dying.

He could still sense Jackson and Tobias moving around him. But he couldn't feel their fists or feet. Nor could he hear their voices over the hissing.

The darkness brightened. Inside became outside. Night became day. The sun burst down on Joe.

He was half-kneeling on a pavement, panting.

For a few seconds, he couldn't think where he was. This was his own world, he knew. But what had he been doing before he slipped into Lucy's time?

Cautiously, he raised his head. The dizziness wasn't as bad as usual. His heart was still hammering, but it was anger he felt rather than fear; anger at what had been done to Amos, by these men and others before them. Fury surged through him, and lifted him to his feet.

15

"You okay, Joe?" Dad had stopped on the pavement ahead. "Was I walking too fast?"

"No, it's fine." Joe stepped carefully forward to join him. The world wasn't lurching as much as it usually did, and he didn't feel sick either. It was as though his anger had given him extra strength. After last time, and all the times before, he felt very grateful. Thank you, Amos, he said silently.

He looked around, trying to get his bearings. Then he remembered: this was Park Street, and he'd been looking for Lucy's house. He and Dad were about to walk up Brandon Hill.

He felt weary at the prospect. Lucy's Bristol was much more firmly fixed in his mind now than it had been before. He didn't need to try and reconstruct it from what he could see in the present. In fact, he didn't want to let the modern city blot out the past so soon.

But Dad was already turning off to the left. Joe blinked. This must be where he'd been, just a few minutes ago, hiding in one of the houses up here. It was crazy! No wonder Lucy thought no-one would believe him! He could scarcely believe it himself!

Yet the anxiety gnawing in his stomach was real enough. What was going to happen to Amos? Tobias and Jackson had to be stopped. But there was absolutely nothing he could do about it!

"That's the Georgian House Museum there, John Pinney's house," Dad said, pointing.

Joe paused to look. He definitely recognised the building, but it wasn't standing on its own any more: a garage had been built on, and more houses added on both sides so that it was now part of a terrace stretching all the way up the road. Opposite, where the trees and graveyard had been, there was a grand church. Joe felt sad, though he couldn't really say why.

"Can I change my mind?" he asked. "Can we go in, after all?"

"Of course," Dad said. They went up the steps.

Inside, Joe halted. He realised he'd been assuming that it would be something like Lucy's house. This wasn't.

The wall of the room on the left had been removed altogether to show Pinney's study. Beyond that, the hallway itself was an odd shape. Nothing was where he expected. Of course, Lucy herself had said these houses were different. But he was still bewildered.

He looked around, trying to steady his mind. It

didn't help that there were other people here, members of staff and other visitors. Their modern clothes jarred against the backdrop. Joe reminded himself that he didn't blend in either. Yet he couldn't shake the feeling that it was everyone else who was out of place.

"Shall we start on this floor?" Dad asked. "Or go down to the kitchens and work our way up?"

Joe bit his tongue to stop himself saying that below stairs was for the servants. "Let's look round here first," he said, hoping that would give him enough time to get over the clash of past and present.

But the clash of past and past bewildered him too. There was a lot here that was really similar to Lucy's home: the kind of furniture, the chandeliers, the tall windows. But the layout was so different. Lucy had been right, too – it was grander, especially the huge withdrawing room on the first floor.

As they went from room to room, Joe felt Lucy's world gradually slipping away from him. By the time they went down to the kitchens, he was firmly back in the present. It was just as well, he supposed. Otherwise, he would really struggle with normal life. All the same, he felt frustrated. If only he could have taken a camera into her time! He thought of all the photos he could have taken with Lucy over the past year and a half. What an album that would make!

Instead, he just had his scars. Standing in the housekeeper's sitting room, he looked down at his palm. The cut from the penknife had virtually disappeared, as he'd known it would. All that remained was a pale line, no thicker than a hair.

Did this mean he'd finished in Lucy's world, he wondered. The scars had come right at the end every other time. He'd never gone back after the injuries had healed. And yet, she still had his St. Christopher. There hadn't been a chance to ask for it back. He pictured her perched on the chair in the withdrawing room, helpless in the face of her father's anger. He hadn't even said goodbye. It couldn't be over! Not yet!

"That was interesting, wasn't it?" Dad said, as they left the museum later. "I know you weren't very keen to look at the stuff on slavery at the M Shed, but I thought the exhibition about Pinney's plantations really added to this experience. I mean, without it, it would have just been another rich man's house."

Joe nodded. It seemed unreal that the M Shed had been only yesterday. So much had happened since then. History hadn't changed, of course. But somehow, he felt better for knowing that William Lucas had seen the way slaves were treated and wanted to stop it.

"I do find it fascinating," Dad went on, "to think how little of this was around when I was a student."

"How do you mean?" Joe asked. "I know Pero's bridge is new, but this house must have been here, and all the rest of the Georgian buildings."

"Of course. But there really wasn't much about Bristol's part in the Slave Trade. This place might have been a museum, but I don't remember anything about

Pero, or about the shameful way that Pinney and the others made their money. The men we now call slave traders used to be referred to as West India merchants, which has rather a different ring to it, don't you think?"

They walked up the street towards Brandon Hill. "That's being put right now, isn't it?" Joe said.

"What's been done is a start, certainly," Dad agreed. "And the debate we were talking about yesterday, about Colston Hall, is a good thing, even if it makes people cross. But I just wonder whether exhibitions and apologies and names of things can ever be enough." He hunched down inside his coat. "It *is* important that people know what Britain did, and who the men on our statues really were. But if we were the descendants of enslaved Africans, would we feel satisfied with a few noticeboards? As though everything's fine as long as there's a display about it?"

Joe frowned.

"That's the problem, you see," Dad said. "You know how passionately I believe in education – of course I do, or I wouldn't have become a teacher. But in this case, I can't help feeling that it's all just talk." He looked up at the sky. "Sometimes," he mused, "I get fed up with the trumpeting that goes on about 'Great' Britain. This country has a pretty chequered past, and a lot of it's not great at all. At the same time as we were trading slaves, we were rampaging across the rest of the globe, taking over other people's countries, trampling the lives of millions and wiping

190

out entire populations with the diseases we took with us. I've often thought that Britain has been really great at oppression! But we've been much less great at making amends."

Joe didn't know what to say.

"A few years ago," Dad went on, "this country celebrated the two hundredth anniversary of the abolition of the Slave Trade – the change in the law that made it illegal. And from the way it was marked, I swear if you were an alien from another planet, you would have thought that Britain had had nothing to do with slavery except for putting a stop to it!

"And 1807 was only the end of the *trade* anyway, not the end of slavery itself. So while the British navy was nobly patrolling the seas, preventing ships from transporting new slaves, out in the West Indies, British planters were still allowed to keep and mistreat the slaves they already had!"

"So abolition wasn't such a great thing after all?" Joe was dismayed. Lucy's father had talked about it as though it would be a really big change. But it sounded like it wouldn't help the slaves he'd left behind in Jamaica.

"It was," Dad corrected him. "Slavery couldn't have been abolished without stopping the trade in slaves first. And we shouldn't forget either that there were people who devoted their whole lives to fighting for it, in the face of defeat after defeat. But the trouble is, their story makes abolition sound like the triumph of white men – one white man, in fact. The only person most people can name is William Wilberforce. He was a good man, no question. And there were other good men too, like Granville Sharp and Thomas Clarkson. And women, like Hannah More. But what about the black campaigners? What about Olaudah Equiano?"

"Who?"

"Exactly! Almost nobody today has heard of him. He was a freed slave who came to England and published his life story in the 1780s. He did a lot to change people's minds about slavery.

"And what about black resistance in the plantations? What about the slaves who refused to work, not because they were lazy, but as a protest? Parts of their bodies were cut off as punishment! And those brave enough to rise up against their white masters were killed! Those people risked much more than anyone here in their fight for freedom.

"But we forget all that and cast them as the victims. We forget that the descendants of slaves are the survivors, born from the strongest and most determined of the millions we took."

Joe heard Amos' voice inside his head. *I can bear more pain, more hatred and anger, than you will ever know. A slave who cannot do that cannot survive.*

"The thing is," Dad was saying, "Wilberforce's story has become a romantic myth: one man against the establishment. The way we tell it, as though every one of us would have done the same, conveniently overlooks the fact that the richest and most powerful Englishmen fought tooth and nail to *keep* slavery. That's why it took another thirty years to stop it after the trade was abolished." Dad paused. "You know what did it in the end? How the government finally pushed it through?"

"How?"

"Compensation."

"You mean, money paid out?" Joe brightened. "Well, that's good, isn't it? I know money isn't everything, but at least the slaves got something!"

"No," Dad said flatly. "The compensation wasn't paid to the slaves. It was paid to their owners."

"What?" Joe was aghast. He thought of Amos. Stolen, sold, cruelly treated, and about to be stolen and sold a second time if Tobias got his way. And if he survived until abolition, it would be the man who bought him who got the money.

"Twenty million pounds," Dad said, "that's how much was paid out to slave owners for their loss of 'property'. That would be about sixteen billion today. And even then, the slaves still had to work for another four years unpaid before they were allowed to walk away, with no money, no possessions to speak of, nothing!"

"But how could the government do that?" Joe was beside himself. "How could they think it was right to pay the owners instead of the slaves?"

"They may not have thought it was right. But they saw there was no other way to get so many powerful men to agree. I was looking up some of the Bristol traders last night. John Pinney's son, Charles, was awarded about twenty five thousand pounds, which would be twenty million today. And there was another Bristol slaver who got around three times that!"

Joe was speechless.

"That's another thing," Dad said. "You'll hear it suggested sometimes that someone should pay financial compensation to the descendants of slaves. It's not an unreasonable idea. But the families of the owners who got paid off aren't likely to want to contribute. They'd say they were legally entitled to the money, and technically, they'd be right. In any case, they already put a lot of it into public institutions like I said to you yesterday."

"What about the British government, then?"

Dad shrugged. "As far as they're concerned, the money's gone, over a century ago."

They had climbed to the top of the hill while Dad was talking. At the summit was a small rockery around a tower that hadn't been there in Lucy's time. Victorian, Dad said. Joe stood with his back to it and looked out over the city. He could see the Georgian houses of Queen Square, but apart from them, everything looked entirely different.

A melancholy weight settled on his shoulders.

Lucy's Bristol had been buried beneath layer upon layer of more recent history. And yet the wounds inflicted in her time hadn't healed properly.

"So what can we do to make things better?" he asked in a small voice.

Dad sighed. "It's hard to know. The injustices of the past are often too complicated to sort out. Sometimes, you just have to look for a better way forward. One thing we can do, I think, is celebrate our differences instead of fearing them. Britain is a diverse country these days, which I think is one of the best things about it. In cities, especially, you can find people from lots of different races, nationalities and religions, all living side by side.

"But unfortunately, there are still plenty of people who are frightened of anyone who's different. Fear makes people suspicious, which makes them unfriendly and unwelcoming. Sometimes it even makes them cruel. That's awful. And it's a huge loss, too, because life is so much richer when you can share other cultures. I'd like you to regard people who are different as interesting. But remember as well that underneath, we're all basically the same. We all want safety, comfort, love, respect and freedom."

Joe buried his hands in his pockets, thinking. Was it fear that drove Tobias and Jackson? Maybe Jackson. But in Tobias' case, the fear had become cruelty, and the cruelty had hardened into hatred, sometime long ago. And now, that hatred had found a focus in Amos. Joe thought again of Tobias and Jackson's scheming. The anxiety in his stomach crawled up into his chest.

It didn't leave him but stayed there, tight around his ribs, for the rest of the day and all the way home in the car. Back at home that night, he lay in bed and tried to make himself relax. But the scar across his palm throbbed. When he woke the next morning, his chest was still tight.

Over the next week, he did forget now and then, distracted by something at school. But then the memory would flash into his mind of Amos slumped against the wall, bloody and broken. And with that memory came a creeping guilt. Was it true, what Jackson had said? Was it his fault that Amos had hit the footman? Jackson had accused him of encouraging Amos, and Amos himself had said almost the same. *You've done enough, you and Miss Lucy. You made me remember who I once was.*

Joe wondered bitterly how things would have turned out if he'd never been there. Lucy wouldn't have known Tobias and Jackson were bullying Amos, so she wouldn't have said anything. Amos himself would probably have put up with it. Perhaps, when he couldn't bear it any longer, he might have run away, as they hoped. He might have made a new life for himself somewhere, as a free man. But because of Joe, he was in danger of being shipped back to the plantations, back to a life of hideous brutality.

Joe could hardly bear to think about it, but he found himself unable to put it completely out of his mind either. Although he knew that time passed at an entirely different speed with Lucy, he was convinced the *Isabella* must have sailed by now. As winter became spring and the trees burst into leaf, he looked up how long the voyage would take, and tried to work out whether Amos and Florence had arrived in the West Indies already. The thought of Rose and Billy's eyes, bright with terror in the dark hull of the ship, hovered on the edge of his dreams. If only he could turn the clock back and make things right somehow!

By Easter, however, he was starting to think that he didn't want to go back to Lucy's world at all. If he stayed in his own time, he need never know what had become of Amos and the others. He might eventually forget about it. Or if he couldn't forget, he might be able to persuade himself that Tobias hadn't gone through with the kidnapping. Maybe everyone was fine. Maybe they were all still living peacefully in Bristol.

Of course, not going back meant leaving Lucy behind for good, since she had his St. Christopher. But he told himself that giving up his dearest friend was the price he had to pay for leading Amos into trouble. He reminded himself that he'd got along fine without her for the first ten and a half years of his life. It was foolish to let himself feel – well, whatever it was he felt – about her, since he would never be able to spend time with her properly in any case. "It's for the best," he told himself sternly, trying to ignore the sick feeling that lived in his stomach now.

On the second Tuesday of the Easter holidays, his friend, Tom, suggested they go to the cinema.

"That's a good idea!" Mum said, when he told her. "What are you going to see?"

"*The Boss Baby*," Joe said, without enthusiasm.

"Is that your kind of thing?" She looked at him curiously.

"I just thought I should go out." He knew Mum had noticed how quiet he'd been, though she hadn't said anything.

"Well, it might be better than it sounds." She grinned. Joe smiled wanly back.

He went with Tom. But he never did find out what the film was like. As the lights dimmed, he glanced across the movie theatre and saw a girl at the end of the row who looked a bit like Lucy. And as he thought this, his ears filled with hissing.

His heart lurched. She had called him! Lucy had called him back!

He closed his eyes, grateful for the near darkness, and for the solidity of the chair around him. Waves of panic and hope swamped him one after another. He gripped the arms of his chair and braced himself for the worst.

16

The next moment, he was standing in utter darkness. It felt like an enclosed space. Presumably this was the half-built house where he'd been before. But he couldn't see anything.

He listened. There was the scrabble of a rat, but no other sound except a snatch of drunken singing from far away.

He felt his way across the room, arms and hands outstretched, sliding his feet over the floor. Nothing blocked his way. He could smell sawn timber, and wood smoke carried on the night air.

As his eyes grew accustomed to the dark, he made out the silhouette of the house next door through a gap in the wall. He turned round to peer at the room. Nothing had changed since last time he was here. He was puzzled. In the weeks that had gone by, there should surely have been windows and doors put in, perhaps plaster on the walls. But nothing?

He crossed to the doorway and went out through

the room where he'd heard Jackson and Tobias talking. The dust on the floor had been disturbed, but that didn't tell him anything. Eventually, he found his way to the window he had climbed in through, and scrambled out of it.

It was brighter outside than indoors. The moon shone high in a silvery sky, casting sharp shadows on the ground. Joe pulled his coat close around him. It was too cold to be high summer. He tried to make out whether the leaves on the trees nearby were tinged with autumn, but he couldn't tell in the moonlight. He looked around without knowing what he was looking for. Nothing he could see had changed at all.

A spark of hope leapt inside him. Was it possible that this was the same night as last time? He didn't dare believe it. It could easily be the next night, and still be too late.

He walked down the track towards Park Street, his footsteps loud in the stillness. Beyond the house next door to John Pinney's was a narrow lane he hadn't noticed before. He was about to cross the top of the lane when he heard the stamp and whinny of a horse.

On instinct, he shrank back into the shadows. The horse stood about halfway down the lane. It was hitched to a cart. A boy waited beside it, holding the reins.

As Joe watched, two hooded figures emerged onto the lane from a building on the left. Joe wondered what was in there. Then he realised: this must be how you got to the coach houses and stables of the houses on Park Street. He tried to work out how far down the hill Lucy lived. Was it possible that the two figures had come out of her father's coach house?

He edged closer, keeping in the shadow cast by a high wall that ran down the right hand side of the lane. There was something furtive about these men, assuming they were men. Each was carrying a bundle wrapped in sacking, the second larger than the first, though neither was apparently heavy. As they dumped them over the side of the cart, Joe thought he heard a whimper. But he was too far away to be sure.

Already the two figures were pulling themselves up beside the boy, who had hopped onto the driver's seat. The cart was coming towards him.

Joe froze. What if the hooded figures were Tobias and Jackson? The smaller bundle could have been Billy and the larger one Rose. They hadn't struggled, but they might have been tied up inside the sacking. If that was true, Florence and Amos were probably in the cart already. He had the chance to save them after all! But not if Tobias caught him first!

Joe's pulse was racing. He sidled as quickly as he dared back along the wall. He wished he hadn't crept so far down the lane. A loose stone skittered away beneath his boot. Joe waited for Tobias to shout. But there was no sound other than hooves and wheels.

He reached the end of the lane and scurried up Great George Street. He threw himself down in the shadow beside Pinney's house.

The cart came out of the lane. Its wheels grated against the stones as it turned the corner away from Joe. As it came to the junction with Park Street, the boy cracked the whip. The horse lurched forward. It clattered away down the hill between the silent houses.

Joe ran down the track after them. He was certain now that he'd just witnessed Tobias and Jackson kidnapping the children and probably Amos and Florence as well. He should have stopped them! He should have tried to prevent the cart from setting off! Except, of course, that the two men would have overpowered him easily. He'd have ended up bundled in with the others.

By the time he reached Park Street, the cart was out of sight. Joe hesitated. Should he try to catch up? That way, he would know where Tobias went. But he couldn't rescue four people alone. He couldn't even rescue the children on his own. He had to get help.

He trotted down to Lucy's house and stood beneath her window. The shutters were closed on the inside. He picked up some pebbles from the road and threw one carefully up at the window. It fell short of the house. He threw another. There was a tiny sound as it grazed the window pane. He threw a third and a fourth, then a whole handful. He waited. *Come on, Lucy*.

Nothing happened.

He picked up more stones and threw them all,

careless now. "Come on! Come on!" he muttered through gritted teeth. The longer it took, the further away Tobias and Jackson would get, and the harder it would be to find them.

Behind the glass, the shutters moved. The window opened. But it wasn't Lucy who looked out.

"What is it?" Katherine hissed. Then, recognising Joe, "You shouldn't be here!"

"I need Lucy!"

"She's asleep."

"She can't be!" Joe's voice came out higher than usual. "She just called me!"

Katherine looked over her shoulder and shook her head. "She's fast asleep. Go away!" She closed the window.

Joe took a step back. How could Lucy be asleep? How had he got here if she hadn't been thinking of him?

He looked down the empty street again. It was too bad. He had to rouse her!

"Lucy!" he shouted. Now that Tobias and Jackson had gone, there was no need to be quiet any more. "Lucy!" He knew he would wake William and Ellen, and probably others too. But he'd need plenty of people awake if he was right about what had happened. And only Lucy would believe him enough to go and check.

"Lucy!"

Her window stayed shut. But the window below

203

opened. William's head appeared in its nightcap. He leaned on the sill with both hands. "What is the meaning of all this noise?" he bellowed.

"Sir!" Joe called, "I was trying to wake Lucy. You need to check Amos' room. And Florence and the children. They've been taken. I'm sure of it!"

Suddenly, he wasn't sure. What if he had made a mistake, and the four of them were all safely asleep?

"What absolute nonsense!" roared Lucy's father. "They're tucked up in their beds, as all God-fearing folk should be!" He glowered at Joe. "I told you to go! Now, make yourself scarce!"

"Please, Sir! I beg you, just make sure Amos is still in the house!"

"Did you not hear me? You're disturbing the entire neighbourhood! Do I have to send for the constable?"

Below, the front door opened. Morley stood there in his dressing gown, his wig askew. In one hand he held a candlestick, in the other a long wooden staff. "You heard the master!" he growled. "Now, go!"

"Please!" Joe pleaded. "I overheard Tobias and Jackson talking about selling Amos and the others on to the *Isabella*!"

"A likely story!" Morley's face was rigid. "We know you're not to be trusted." He started down the steps, brandishing the stick. Joe backed away.

Behind Morley, something pale moved. Lucy was in the doorway.

"Please, Lucy!" Joe cried. "Run to Amos and Florence's rooms! I think they've been taken."

Morley's stick was raised above his head now. "Happy now?" The butler's usual mask of civility was quite gone. "You've got what you wanted, and woken up half the street into the bargain!" He advanced on Joe. "Let this be a lesson to you not to do such a thing again!" He brought the stick down hard across Joe's shoulders.

The blow sent a shock wave through Joe. He staggered and fell to his knees. Morley raised the stick again. Joe put his arms over his head. All he could think was, *Hold on! Stay here! Don't let him beat you back into your own time!* Morley cracked the stick down a second time. Joe crumpled.

There was a shout from above. "Stop, man! Stop!" Joe didn't dare look up.

"The boy's right!" William shouted. "They've gone, and so has Tobias! Send someone for the constable, quick! Tell him we'll meet him at the quay."

Morley hurried into the house without a backward look. Joe knelt in the dirt beside the road, massaging his bruised flesh. Of all the people he might have expected to be beaten by, it would not have been Morley! He touched a tender spot and winced. At least the message had got through. He hauled himself up.

A minute later, a boy came out of the servants' entrance and sprinted off down Park Street. For a good while, nobody else came out of the house. With the shutters closed at every window, there was no sign of light. Joe started to wonder whether they were coming after all.

But at last, William appeared with Peter and Morley, each of them carrying a lantern. A sword hung from William's waist.

"What about Lucy?" Joe asked tentatively.

"This is no time for women and children!" William replied.

But they hadn't yet reached College Green when they heard footsteps behind them.

"Go home, child!" William told his daughter, without breaking his stride.

"No, Father." Lucy was breathless but her jaw was set. "If I hadn't believed Joe and gone to look, you wouldn't know they'd gone." She hurried along next to him. "Joe knew already what Tobias and Jackson were up to. He'd seen what they were doing to Amos. He tried to get Amos to tell you. But Amos said he was just a slave."

Unease passed across William's face. But all he said was, "Very well. Come, if you must."

They moved quickly and quietly along the edge of College Green. As they neared the quay, the gracious town houses gave way to older dwellings, tumbled one on top of another. Joe heard a baby crying, and a man shouting. But most people seemed to be asleep.

A few moments later, however, Joe heard the

sounds of hushed activity: the rattle of barrels rolled over cobbles, the hollow sound as they reached the gangplank; the squeaking of ropes being tightened; short, sharp shouts. Water slapped against wood and stone. The tide was high.

With a clutch of his heart, Joe knew what that meant. "Jackson and Tobias wanted to get Amos and Florence onto the *Isabella*!" He seized Lucy's arm. "It's about to leave, isn't it?"

"Is he planning to have them transported back to the plantations?" William sounded alarmed. He quickened his pace. "Constable!" He raised his arm.

Ahead of them, a figure detached itself from the outline of the ship. Joe gazed up. The *Isabella* was huge. In the moonlight, her three masts seemed to soar high overhead, with lines of rope suspended like vast spiders' webs. The ghostly bulk of sail was bunched along each spar, and in the rigging, the silhouettes of a dozen boys stood out against the sky.

In front of the ship, four large rowing boats had been manoeuvred into position. Ropes were now flung out from the ship, with cries of "Make fast!" One oarsman from each boat attached a rope, while the rest huddled on their benches waiting, rubbing their hands to keep warm as swirls of mist rose from the river.

"Mr Lucas, Sir." The constable approached. "You've lost some runaway slaves, I hear."

"Not runaways, Stanford!" William was impatient. "Four Negroes – a man and woman, and a girl and boy – taken from their beds as they slept."

Constable Stanford's eyebrow flicked up. "What makes you think that? And why should they be down here and not on the road to London already?"

William's impatience turned to irritation. "They've been kidnapped by my nephew."

The constable's expression opened up into fascinated astonishment. "How do you know, Sir?"

"I heard him planning it," Joe interrupted. "Please, there's no time to lose! Will the *Isabella* sail tonight?"

"Within the half hour, I'm told," Stanford said pompously.

"Then we have to hurry!" Joe cried. "They'll be on board the ship. They have to be!" He began to move towards it.

"Hold on, young man!" The constable caught him by the shoulder. Joe gasped as the man gripped him just where Morley's stick had struck. "You can't just board a ship, especially not when it's about to sail, unless you fancy visiting the West Indies, of course!" He chortled.

"I don't think you appreciate how serious the situation is," William cut in. "My nephew is known to have been plotting with a former servant from my household. They hope to sell the Negroes for their own gain."

"A former servant, you say?" Constable Stanford clicked his tongue. "Well now, that can't be allowed, theft of the master's property."

William grimaced. But Joe wanted to shake the constable. What did it matter who'd planned the thing? There were people's lives at stake. If they didn't get a move on, it would be too late!

"All the same, we can't just march on board," Stanford said. "We'll need to notify the harbour master and the water bailiff. And the law may require you to get a writ of *Habeas Corpus*."

"Then the law's an ass!" William declared. "If we don't rescue these people now, they'll be gone, and that will be that!" He pushed past Stanford and strode along the quay towards the gangplank of the *Isabella*, just as a figure hurried off the ship.

"Look where you're going please, Sir!" William admonished him. Then he saw the man's face beneath his hood. "Well, well, if it isn't John Jackson!" He caught the footman by the arm before he could slide away. "Would you like to explain what you're doing getting off the *Isabella* at this hour?"

Jackson cringed. "I was on my way to your house, Mr. Lucas, Sir! I was coming to tell you that your slaves have been taken. That boy who claimed to be your nephew from France, he kidnapped them, revenge for you sending him away. Not that you weren't right to do so, Mr. Lucas, Sir!"

William glanced at Joe. Then he said to Jackson, "That's kind of you indeed, though it doesn't explain how you know about it, nor why you're here. Never mind. As you're so anxious to see the culprit brought to justice, you'll be pleased that he's with me." He gestured towards Joe. "We've just been speaking to Constable Stanford, in fact."

Jackson looked at Joe. The colour drained from his face. He wrenched his arm free of William's grasp, and scurried away, his cloak flapping behind him.

William turned to Joe. "That wasn't quite the reaction I expected," he said, perplexed. "Still, there's no time to talk about it now. At least we know that Amos and the others are on the ship. We just have to find them before it leaves."

He marched up the gangplank with everyone else close behind.

"This ship's about to set sail!" shouted a sailor from the deck. "Stay on the quay if you don't want to go with her!"

"I'll take my chance!" William shouted back. He turned to the others. "I'm going to find Captain Roper. I'll wager he knows something about this. In the meantime, Morley, you go down and search the main deck; the rest of you search the lower deck."

He set off towards the stern of the ship. Morley looked around for a moment, then followed a sailor down through a hatch in the deck. Peter went after him.

Joe and Lucy looked at each other. There was so much Joe wanted to say, but he knew it would have to wait. "I've missed you," he mumbled, and then blushed furiously.

Lucy smiled. "It's only been a few hours! I know it was an awful scene earlier this evening. And I'm sorry I couldn't stop my father sending you away. But I was going to try again to persuade him tomorrow. I hoped you wouldn't have gone far."

Joe held up his healed hand. "I've been gone altogether, for weeks," he said.

She stared. "You really have! Goodness ..."

"I'll tell you about it later," he said. "But first, we have to find Amos and Florence."

He followed Morley and Peter down the ladder beneath the hatch. From above, he heard a series of shouts across the upper deck. Lucy looked round.

"Oh no!" she cried. "They're taking up the gangplank! They're raising the sails at the bow!" She rushed away out of Joe's view. Orders were barked out all over the ship.

She reappeared at the top of the ladder. "They've pushed off," she said desperately. "The rowing boats are towing us out. We're moving!"

17

Joe looked up through the hatch at the panic on his friend's face. "What do we do?" she cried.

"Find Amos and the others," Joe answered. "It might be too late to get them off onto the quay. But we can always swim for it!"

Lucy climbed down the ladder. Her feet were shaking. "I can't swim," she whispered.

Joe gulped. This hadn't occurred to him. "Don't worry," he said. "We'll think of something."

They looked around. A lantern swung from the low ceiling. Shadows crowded in around the circle of light. There was no-one down here as far as they could see, though Morley must be somewhere nearby.

Suddenly, the hatch above them slammed shut. Joe and Lucy both jumped. The shadows jumped too, as the lantern shuddered. From the upper deck, they heard cursing. "I think maybe we were supposed to close the hatch," Joe said, with a nervous laugh.

With the hatch shut, it was dimmer than ever

down here. Everything was wooden. It was like being in a log cabin, except that the sides of the ship were curved. A column as big as a tree trunk came up through the floor and went out through the ceiling. Lines of rope were taut down one side of it. Joe noticed another column further along. These must be two of the masts. More timbers held up the deck above and there were wooden crates and giant coils of rope.

"Where now?" Lucy asked.

"Down another level, I think." They opened a hatch at their feet and climbed down a second ladder, closing the hatch behind them this time.

The lower deck was even more cramped. The timbers holding up the main deck were shorter, so the ceiling wasn't far above their heads. The trunk-like masts came down through here too, and either side of the nearest one was a pair of cannons, pointing outwards.

"Why have they got guns?" Joe asked, alarmed. "I thought this was a merchant ship?"

"Protection from pirates, I suppose," Lucy said.

Between the guns hung rows of hammocks. "I guess this is where the crew sleep." Joe made a face. "No hiding anything here."

From beyond the hammocks came the sound of someone moving around.

"Is that you, Peter?" Lucy's voice quavered.

"I can't find them," her brother called softly. Joe could hear him making his way back towards them.

"I've looked everywhere!"

"Sssssh!" Joe cocked his head. "Voices! Can you hear them?"

All three of them listened. From beneath their feet came the sound of an argument.

"Is there another deck down there?" Peter asked.

"I don't think so," Joe said. "But there's the hold isn't there, where they store the cargo?"

They peered around in the gloom. "How do we get down there?" Lucy wondered.

Suddenly, a hatch flew open a little further along. A greasy looking man scrambled out of it. He stopped abruptly at the sight of Joe, Lucy and Peter. "I thought you said you weren't followed!" he snapped over his shoulder.

"We weren't!" retorted a voice from below.

"So how do you explain this lot 'ere? They don't look like sailors to me." The man lunged past Joe and Lucy, grabbing the next ladder. "You're on your own!" he snarled down. "False pretences, that's what I'd call this!" With that, he pushed up the hatch overhead and vanished onto the main deck.

Tobias' face appeared beneath the gap in the floor. Seeing Lucy and Peter, he cursed and kicked something. There was a cry of pain.

Joe sprang forward, jerked into action by the sound. "They're down there, aren't they?" The anger he'd felt last time he saw Tobias crackled through him. *This time*, he thought! *This time, I will get you!*

214

He leapt through the gap, not bothering with the ladder, and landed on his feet below.

Tobias staggered backwards. His face had turned ashen, just like Jackson's. "What are you doing here?" His voice trembled. "You disappeared under my hands! Are you a ghost?"

"I've come back for you!" Joe yelled. "And *them!*" He flung out his arm towards Amos and the others, who were huddled, still bound and gagged, against a stack of barrels. "You're not getting away with this!"

He didn't wait for Tobias to gather himself together, but threw himself at him. "I hate you!" he shouted. He smashed his fist into Tobias' jaw. Tobias' head flew back with a satisfying crack. A feeling of immense power surged through Joe.

"I hate you for what you are, and what you believe!" He punched Tobias again. "I hate men like you who kidnap innocent people, even children!" Joe pounded out his words with his fists. Still his fury grew. "You think it's alright to imprison them!" Another punch. "You think it's alright to treat them worse than animals! You think it's alright if they die!"

At once, everything Dad had told him, everything William had seen, everything he had witnessed himself, came together into one dark point. He thought of the children bundled up in sacking, of Amos collecting broken china with scalded hands, of Florence weeping over Amos' bleeding body.

215

Rage towered inside Joe like nothing he had ever felt in his life. His fists opened into claws. He bared his teeth. He struck out with his feet. "You should pay for what you've done to them!" he screeched. "You don't deserve to live!"

Behind him, he sensed movement. But he couldn't stop now. He wanted to kill Tobias. He knew he would actually do it! The violence of his desire terrified him. But he had to go on!

Then strong hands pulled him away. "Enough," William said. "Enough, young man!"

Lucy's father held Joe until he stopped thrashing against him, then steered him firmly to one side. Joe was shaking from head to toe. Fury was still blazing through him, so intense he could hardly see.

He turned around.

Lucy had freed Rose and was untying the ropes that bit into Billy's wrists and ankles. Peter had loosened the gags across the mouths of all four, and was now using William's sword to cut Amos and Florence free. Rose's eyes gleamed white, like beacons of panic.

Joe fell to his knees and flung his arms around her neck. He hugged her tightly, as though he could make everything alright. "I'm sorry!" he choked. "I'm so sorry!" He didn't really know why he was saying it. Sorry for frightening her, perhaps. But it was more than that. Sorry for everything else, everything that had happened to her and all the others everywhere.

216

As he clung to her, he felt her arms uncurl. Her small hand stroked his hair. Her neck was damp. The tears were his, he realised. He was sobbing.

A hand touched his arm. He raised his head. "It's alright, Joe." Lucy crouched beside him. "It's going to be alright." They stood up.

Tobias was also on his feet now, facing William. One eye had swelled up, and his top lip was thick from Joe's attack.

"What were you thinking, Tobias?" William's voice was low and menacing. "That you'd sell them? Make some money?"

Tobias didn't answer.

"Captain Roper wants nothing to do with it," William said. "Not that he's a moral man! He just doesn't want the cost of feeding them. He doesn't want the risk either. What if they die on the way, he said, or fetch a lower price than you expected him to pay?"

"He's a fool!" snorted Tobias. "They're fit and well. It won't take much to keep them alive, and then they'll fetch a good sum! Plenty enough for both of us!"

Joe saw William struggle to control his temper. "Only when they reach the West Indies!" he answered. "Were you planning to take them there yourself?"

Tobias thrust out his chin in defiance.

"You weren't, were you? You were hoping to get someone else to do your dirty work! Was it that unpleasant man who burst out of the hatch in front of

217

me just now? Who was he, a slave-catcher?" William's lip curled. "You weren't expecting him to take them to Jamaica, surely? Did you think he'd get a higher price for you? I'm guessing that didn't work out either." Lucy's father scoffed. "You really hadn't thought this through!"

Tobias glared at him.

"Did you not know how slave-catchers make most of their money?" William asked. "They collect the rewards offered by the owners of runaway slaves. *I* would have had to pay *him* for bringing these four back. You were a fool if you thought he'd pay you *and* take them away!"

Still Tobias was silent.

"He got quite wet getting off the ship," William said. There was bitter amusement in his tone. "You'll need to keep out of his way when we get home!"

"Home!" Tobias spat. "Your house isn't my home! England's not my home! Now that this ship has set sail, I'm staying on it."

"Really?" William studied him. "And how exactly are you going to pay for your passage? You can't possibly think I'll let you take Amos and the others with you, to sell in the West Indies."

Tobias narrowed his eyes. "Admit it, Uncle," he said, "you'd be glad to see the back of me. Why not pay Captain Roper to take me off your hands?"

William gave a bray of mirthless laughter. "Impudent boy! You're right, I can't wait for you to be gone. But I'm not paying for the pleasure! You can see if Roper will let you work your passage as an extra hand. But he won't pay you, and it won't be an easy crossing – his temper is famous!"

"I'm not afraid," rumbled Tobias. "I've done it before, remember?"

"You were a boy of ten." William sniffed. "A lot more will be expected of you this time. And don't forget, you'll need to find somewhere else to live when you arrive. The plantation is being sold."

Tobias looked daggers at him.

"In fact, that's not all," William said, with satisfaction. "Your mother agrees that if we make enough money to clear the debts without selling all of the slaves, we'll give the rest their freedom."

"You can't do that!" shrieked Tobias. "They're my property!"

"Not yet, they're not. You may think you're a man, but in the eyes of the law, you're a child till you turn twenty-one. Until then, you can't stop me."

"That's outrageous!"

William shrugged. "I intend to make provision for the two children," he said, glancing at Billy and Rose, "and I was going to do the same for you, even though I'd much rather not. But I will only treat you as family if you come back with us now. If you choose to leave, you'll have to fend for yourself, for good."

Two bright spots appeared high up on Tobias' cheeks. "That's blackmail!" he cried. His eyes flashed.

"Not really." William brushed some dust off the sleeve of his coat. "You do have a genuine choice. Now," he became brisk, "I need to get the rest of us, including your hostages, safely back to dry land. If you'd like to join us –"

"Go to hell!" thundered Tobias. "And you too!" he added, looking first at Amos and then at Joe. His hands clenched into fists.

"Don't you dare touch either of them," warned William.

Tobias picked up his lantern and scaled the ladder. At the top, he paused. "You might think you've won, but it's not over yet!" He stepped out of the hatch and slammed it shut, shooting the bolt home.

Darkness filled the hold. Joe heard a sharp intake of breath. Billy and Rose both began to cry.

"Have courage, little ones," William said quietly. "All is not lost."

Joe reached out towards Lucy. She took his hand and held it tight. They stood together, side by side in the dark, and waited.

A few minutes later, they heard voices above. The bolt was scraped back. The hatch opened. Morley and one of the sailors peered down at them.

"Ready?" William asked.

"Yes, Sir," Morley replied.

"Very good. Lucy and Joe, you climb out first." William turned to help Florence to her feet. "Can you do this?" he asked gently. "Or were you hurt?"

"I am well, Massa," she answered.

"Then we'll help the children out behind you."

After that, it was Amos' turn. Joe and Lucy stood on the lower deck watching as William and Peter helped Amos up the ladder and out through the hatch. He looked frail and exhausted, his movement was awkward, his face still swollen with bruising. The cut to his lip had opened again, and blood encrusted his mouth. But there was something in his expression that Joe hadn't seen before.

He didn't speak, but as he stood on the lower deck in the lamplight, he put out his hand to Joe. His shirt was torn and his wrists were grazed from the ropes that had tied him.

Joe went to him. And Amos wrapped Joe in his arms, squeezing him so hard that Joe could barely breathe. For a second time, emotion rose in Joe's throat, choking him.

On the upper deck, beneath the bright moon, the group huddled together for warmth. A strange collection they made: a white gentleman in fine clothes supporting a broad-shouldered black man; two young black children and a woman, all in their nightshirts; and close around them three well-dressed white children.

Morley stood a little distance away, talking to the sailor. "When we reach the mouth of the Avon," the sailor was saying, "that's your chance, while we're setting the square sails. Two to a boat, I'd say, except for the little ones, who can go with their nursemaid."

Morley nodded. "Can the boats come right up to the hull?"

The sailor rubbed finger and thumb together.

"Yes, yes!" Morley said impatiently. "It's going to be an expensive business, I see that. But we have to get us all safely back to shore! Is that the rope ladder there?"

"All will be well, Morley," William interrupted. "Don't fuss." He gazed out over the bow of the ship. All was quiet except for the chop and splash of the oars as the boats tugged the ship steadily towards the river mouth. Between the wooded hillsides ahead lay the sea.

Joe felt calm at last. But through that calm, he was keenly aware of Lucy beside him. He wanted to take her hand again, as he had done in the darkness. But he didn't dare. "My St. Christopher," he murmured, "have you still got it?"

She put her hand to her neck. "I put it on before I came out, for good luck. It's strange – I usually keep it under my pillow at night, but it was in my hand when your shouting woke us." She paused, then said, "You know what? I've just remembered, I had the most vivid dream about you!"

Joe grinned.

"Why are you smiling? You don't know what I dreamt!"

"It doesn't matter what happened in your

dream," Joe said. "All that matters is that you dreamed it."

Lucy frowned.

"Your aunt told me you were asleep," Joe said. "I couldn't understand it. I couldn't see how you'd called me back. But if you were holding the St. Christopher, your dream must have been enough!"

She nodded. "Do you want to take it now?"

"I probably should," Joe said reluctantly. "But you do realise what that means?"

"That you can't come back?" Her face fell. "But everything's going to be so much better now! Josiah has gone, Tobias too, and I'm sure my father would let you stay after what you did tonight – wouldn't you, Father?"

William looked round vaguely. "What's that?"

"Let Joe stay after all?"

"I dare say that would be alright." He spoke a little gruffly, but his eyes were kind. "After all, it's thanks to you, Joe, that I still have my 'property'."

"About that, Sir," Joe ventured.

"No need to say it, young man," William interrupted him. "As I was talking to the constable tonight, I realised there's unfinished business with Amos and Florence. It pained me to hear him speak of them as slaves, and to refer to them as property. I haven't thought of them as such since we returned to England together. But how can I talk of freeing slaves from the plantation when Amos and Florence are still

223

considered by others to be owned by our family?"

He turned to the manservant and nursemaid. "In a few minutes," he said, "we will leave this ship in the boats below. They will take us back to shore, and I'll arrange carriages home for all of us.

"When I say home, I mean my home. It shall also be your home if you choose. But from the moment your feet touch the shore, Amos, Florence, I wish to make it clear that you are free – free to choose where and how you live, the work you do, who you love. As free as the rest of us."

He looked down at Billy and Rose. "My sister-in-law, Katherine, intends to adopt the children. We will look after them together, as though they were our own. For their sake, as well as mine, I hope you will choose to be employed in my household, Florence, as a free woman, at least until the children are more settled. I believe Sarah is about to leave, in case that helps.

"As for you, Amos, although I value your loyal service to me, you are capable of much more. I'm not so selfish as to keep you from what you could become! As soon as you are well enough, we will teach you to read and write. Then we'll seek out a suitable apprenticeship together, so that you can learn a trade of your own."

Astonished silence greeted this announcement. Then, "Thank you, Master," Amos and Florence said softly together.

Joe looked at Amos. He'd expected a more dramatic reaction than this. But he saw on Amos' face a kind of dazed relief. There was no doubt that he understood the meaning of William's words.

The ship had now reached the mouth of the river. Before them, moonlight fell across the sea like a silver road leading away to the horizon. It was so bright, it was as though you could hear it whispering to you, Joe thought, through the waves and the wind. He stood beside Lucy, looking out. The whispering grew.

Joe's heart fell like a stone. It wasn't the sound of the sea. On impulse, he took hold of Lucy's hand again. She looked at him in surprise. But she must have read in his eyes what was happening, because she pulled her hand away, unfastened the St. Christopher and gave it to him.

Then she took his hand again. "Is this it?" she breathed. "You've done what you had to do, and now you're going?"

He nodded miserably. Already the sea was disappearing into a mist that hadn't been there a few moments ago.

"I wish …" He didn't know how to finish, didn't really know what he did wish. He didn't want more lessons with Miss Waters. He didn't want to fall into the routine of Lucy's life. He would miss his own life too much.

"I wish I could take you back with me," he said.

She smiled sadly. "I don't know how I'd manage in your time. This is where I belong. This is my world." She was fading out, growing fainter.

"This time it is," he replied. He clutched her hand more tightly. But he couldn't really feel it now. She was slipping away. Or he was. "But next time, you'll be somewhere else. As long as –"

But she was gone. They were all gone, Lucy, William, Amos, and the rest. The moonlight had dimmed. The ship had melted away.

"As long as there is a next time," Joe finished.

"What was that?" Tom leaned over from the seat next to him.

Bright colours and loud music blared out of the cinema screen. Joe closed his eyes and put his hands over his ears. It was too much! He got to his feet and stumbled out.

"Are you ill?" Tom asked, coming out a couple of minutes later to find him sitting on the stairs.

Joe shook his head. "No, I feel much better actually. I'm just not in the mood for this today. I think I'll go home."

"Shall I come with you?"

"No. You go and watch the film. You may as well. I'll see you later."

See you later, he thought as he walked back to his house. He wished he could have said that to Lucy. Would he see her later? There were still over two hundred years of history before the present day. So

226

there was bound to be a later, wasn't there? He didn't want to go right now. He just wanted to know that he would, some time.

He looked down at the fine white line across the palm of his hand. It was comforting somehow to have the scars as an indelible record of the time he'd spent with Lucy. But whilst they remained on the surface of his skin, Lucy herself seemed to be getting more and more deeply embedded inside him. Just thinking about her made his chest feel light.

But what was the use? He kicked a stone in frustration. Even if he saw her later, in another world, then what? Another life, another few days together, another scar. It could never be enough!

He sighed. For now, in any case, there was nothing to be done. His St. Christopher was back in his pocket. All he could do was wait. Wait and see if there was a later, and when that might turn out to be. Wait and see what his friend might mean to him when he got there. Wait and see, and hope, that maybe, just maybe, there might, one day, be some way of holding on.

THE END

227

The Brookes Slave Ship

The diagram below shows how the Brookes slave ship carried 454 slaves, confining each adult slave to a space just 40cm in width. Before the law imposed this limit on the number of slaves carried, the Brookes previously carried as many as 609 slaves.

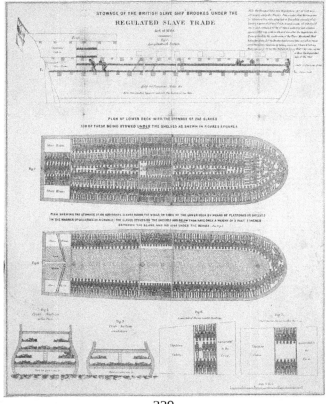

Lightning Source UK Ltd.
Milton Keynes UK
UKOW04f2203170118
316336UK00001B/2/P